# No More Lies

## Priceless Revenge
### Book 3

### Roxy Sloane

Roxy Sloane Books

Copyright © 2022 by AAHM Inc/Roxy Sloane

All rights reserved.

No part of this book may be reproduced in any form or by any electronic or mechanical means, including information storage and retrieval systems, without written permission from the author, except for the use of brief quotations in a book review.

Cover design by British Empire Designs

❦ Created with Vellum

# Also by Roxy Sloane:

**THE OXFORD LEGACY TRILOGY:**
1. Cross My Heart
2. Break My Rules
3. Seal My Fate

**THE FLAWLESS TRILOGY:**
(Caleb & Juliet)
1. Flawless Desire
2. Flawless Ruin
3. Flawless Prize

**THE RUTHLESS TRILOGY:**
(Nero & Lily)
1. His Ruthless Heart
2. These Ruthless Games
3. Our Ruthless Vow

**THE PRICELESS REVENGE TRILOGY:**
(Sebastian & Avery)
1. Dig Two Graves
2. One Dark Secret
3. No More Lies

THE SEDUCTION SERIES:
1. The Seduction
2. The Bargain
3. The Invitation
4. The Release
5. The Submission
6. The Secret
7. The Exposé
8. The Reveal

THE TEMPTATION DUET:
1. One Temptation
2. Two Rules

THE KINGPIN DUET:
1. Kingpin
2. His Queen

Explicit: A Standalone Novel

Priceless Revenge: Book Three

No More Lies

***Revenge is priceless…*** Discover the final book in the spicy, thrilling new trilogy from USA Today bestselling author Roxy Sloane!

They say when a man embarks on revenge, he should dig two graves.

But what about a woman?

I swore I'd destroy Sebastian Wolfe, no matter the cost. I surrendered my innocence - and my heart. But now, his secrets could be both our undoing.

Is he the monster I've been chasing?

Or the only man who can save me?

THE PRICELESS REVENGE TRILOGY:

(Sebastian & Avery)

1. Dig Two Graves

2. One Dark Secret

3. No More Lies

## Chapter 1

## *Avery*

"Sebastian!" I scream as a deafening explosion suddenly tears through the small private jet. We lurch dangerously, mid-air, and to my horror, I see flames out of one window, the right wing crumpled and going up in smoke.

"Hold on!" he yells, covering me with his body, protecting me as the plane shakes and dips.

"What do we do?" I cry, as Sebastian stumbles back into the pilot's seat.

"Sit down and buckle up!" he yells at me, trying to get control of the plane again. "We have to do an emergency landing!"

Oh God. I do what he says, fumbling with the belt in panic. I can see the dark mountains rearing up ahead of us, the snowy forests barely lit by our flashes of light. They're coming too fast. Too close. "Sebastian!" I scream again, as we plow into the forest, the sound of crunching glass and metal deafening as the crushing impact sends me reeling.

And everything goes black.

. . .

"Avery. Avery, wake up."

I moan in protest, eyes squeezed shut and my head pounding.

"Come on, Avery!"

Sebastian's voice is too loud, and now something is shaking me. My eyelids flutter, letting in light that's too bright, and I groan, trying to turn away.

It hurts. Everything hurts.

"Go 'way," I mumble, needing to sleep again. God, sleep, it's all I want. Just to drift off, gently, into the haze of darkness beckoning me—

CRACK.

Someone slaps me across the face. Hard.

My eyes fly open, and I gasp in shock. "What the hell?" I demand, finding Sebastian leaning over me. His jaw is bruised. His eyes are dark as he grips my face in both hands.

"Avery." His flash of relief is gone so fast, I could be imagining it.

"I can't believe you just slapped me," I blurt, my head still ringing.

"You needed to wake up. Now you are. Are you hurt?" He asks briskly, releasing me.

"I..." I look around, taking in the crumpled metal and broken glass around me. The jet is on its side in the snow, the windows of the cockpit smashed, and snow billowing in.

I shiver, with shock—and the cold.

"Focus," Sebastian barks. "Are you hurt? Can you stand?"

I swallow hard, trying to pull myself together despite the fear and confusion whirling in my mind. *The explosion... Our crash landing...*

We survived.

"I'm OK, I think," I venture. My head is still pounding, and I reach my hand up, wincing when I brush against a cut near my hairline. I pull my fingertips away and see blood.

Sebastian immediately examines it. "The cut's not deep. You'll be fine."

Fine.

It's not a word I'd use right now, crash-landed somewhere in the Swiss Alps, alone with a man who was just pledging to make me suffer.

Destroy me the way I'd destroyed him.

Now, Sebastian unbuckles the belt digging into my stomach, and offers me his hand to help me up.

I hesitate. A few hours ago, I revealed his darkest secrets to the world—that he was responsible for the car crash that killed his father and another driver. He was led off in handcuffs, his reputation ruined, removed from his billion-dollar company like the monster he is.

I took everything from him.

And Sebastian Wolfe isn't a man to just forgive and forget, no matter how dire our situation is right now.

He gives a bitter laugh, seeing the reluctance in my stare. "Fine."

Sebastian turns away from me and climbs through into the cabin, leaving me alone in the wreckage of the cockpit.

*Fuck.*

There's no way out of this, not without him, so I pull myself upright—

Bad idea.

The world spins. I have to grab the back of my seat to steady myself, until finally, my dizziness passes, and I awkwardly climb back after Sebastian. He's rummaging through the wreckage, and I take in the destruction, standing on what was the jet wall. The small cabin is like a disaster zone;

pieces of a doll's house flung around. All the windows are broken and the side of the plane where the explosion happened is gone. I peek out of the gaping fuselage and take stock of our surroundings.

Snowy mountain peaks. Thick forest. An icy blue sky.

That's it. As far as the eye can see: white, and dark green, and glaring sun. There's nothing else in sight.

*Nobody* else.

"Where are we?" I ask, as fear claws, cold in my chest.

"The Alps." Sebastian replies, not looking up. He's heaving the leather seats up, searching for something in the mess of metal and glass.

My feeling of disorientation grows. "Switzerland?"

I try to remember the little flight path map from takeoff. Lake Como to London, over the mountains. We'd only just hit cruising altitude when the engine exploded; we couldn't have gotten far.

"What are you looking for?" I ask, rubbing my arms with my hands. I'm freezing.

He doesn't answer, rifling through the overhead bins now—which aren't overhead anymore, they're on the ground.

"What are we going to do? What caused the crash?" I continue with the questions, growing more and more panicked when he doesn't answer. I wish I knew where my phone was. I'd left it in a seat, and it could have ended up anywhere during the landing. "Have you called for help?"

"Here."

Sebastian finally turns to face me, and he's holding out a coat. The thick red parka looks huge, and I snatch it out of his hands without hesitation and pull it on, thankful for the immediate warmth.

"How long will it take for rescue to arrive?" I ask as he finds my suitcase and shoves it over to me.

"They're not coming. Do you have any boots?"

His words are matter-of-fact. I freeze in place, staring at him.

"What are you talking about?" I ask, my heart pounding in fear again.

"Boots. Shoes. Anything you can walk in—better than those," he adds with a sneer, nodding at the flimsy sandals still strapped to my feet.

When I don't move, he scowls. "Avery, we don't have time for this. Get dressed, as warm as you can. We have a long hike ahead of us."

"Where to?" I exclaim, gesturing out at the endless snowy vista. "There's nothing *there*! No," I say, determined. "I saw a documentary once, about a plane going down. The people who went wandering off into the wilderness didn't make it. We should stay here and wait for rescue."

I heave a seat upright and sit myself down with a stubborn glare.

"I told you." Sebastian clenches his jaw. "No one's coming to find us."

"Of course they will," I argue. "There's a black box! We've disappeared from radar! They already know we're in distress, and when the plane doesn't arrive in London as planned, they'll come looking—"

"And they won't find us!"

Sebastian's yell echoes in the wreckage of the cabin. I flinch back, watching as he drags a hand through his hair, full of tension. "They won't find us, because I planned it that way."

"I don't understand..." I stare at him, trying to make sense of it.

"I told you, I took a detour so you and me could talk. I turned off the flight communicator so nobody could track us," Sebastian says curtly. "We're hundreds of miles off our official flight plan. Nobody's coming to rescue you, because nobody knows where the fuck we are!"

His words sink in.

I let out a hysterical laugh. "You mean... Because you were kidnapping me, we're going to freeze to death out here? That's just perfect," I say, giving him a slow clap. "Amazing work. Truly, that's the genius planning and strategy I would expect from the great Sebastian Wolfe."

He glares. "You should be thanking me," Sebastian growls, finding a duffel bag in the wreckage that must be his own luggage.

"Thanking you?" I echo in disbelief.

"Yes. Because if we'd been on the official flight plan, that explosion would have crashed us down in the middle of nowhere. Instead, we're about twenty miles from my lodge. We can make it by nightfall, but only if we start walking now." He hefts his bag and climbs through the gaping hole in the side of the cabin, out into the snow.

He pauses to look back at me impatiently. "Avery, I'm not fucking around here. We need to go. Now."

I don't move. "I wouldn't go anywhere with you if my life depended on it."

"Fine." Sebastian scowls. "It's your choice. Stay here and freeze. Or maybe the wolves will get you first."

He starts to walk, trudging determinedly in the snow— without once looking back.

I watch him go, his figure getting smaller and smaller, further away.

Leaving me here alone. With no food, no warmth, no chance of rescue. No hope of surviving the night.

It's either Sebastian or the wolves.

*Damn it.*

I quickly unbuckle my sandals and switch them out for a

pair of boots in my case. Rifling through the rest of my things, I grab a wool hat and a scarf. I wasn't exactly dressing for the snow, but I do the best I can. Then, I gather some clothes and a few other essentials, cramming them into my shoulder bag before climbing awkwardly out of the plane after Sebastian.

"Wait!" I call out, struggling to catch up as my feet sink into the snow. "Sebastian!"

He doesn't stop, but he slows a little, until I finally draw level with him. "How far is it?" I ask, fastening my coat tighter. The sun is still high in the sky, but the mountains are looming, snowy, all around us, and the silence is ominous, filling me with unease.

Sebastian doesn't reply.

"I said, how far?" I try again, hating that I'm stuck with him.

"I don't know, five hours' walk north, maybe six," Sebastian says, checking his expensive watch. It turns out, there's some kind of compass on the watch face, and he adjusts direction, pointing to the narrow passage between two mountain peaks. "If we follow the valley, we should hit a road eventually."

"And then?"

"Then we pray we make it before nightfall."

I gulp. "My ankle hurts," I say, feeling the ache with every step. "I don't think I can walk for that long."

Sebastian sends me a scornful look. "You can take it."

His reply is like a sharp slap, mocking me with the same words he groaned in passion. How I loved hearing his filthy orders.

How I begged for more.

The shame ricochets through me, mingling with my fear and fury, until I can't see straight.

I stop walking. "You think this is funny?"

Sebastian keeps walking. My fury builds.

"This isn't a joke!" I scream, my voice echoing in the empty valley. I charge after him, suddenly incensed by his cool composure. Reaching him, I shove hard at his back. "None of this is funny!"

Caught by surprise, Sebastian stumbles, almost losing his footing in the snow.

"People are dead because of you!" I yell, the terror and tension boiling over. "Does that mean anything?"

Sebastian sneers at me. "You mean, like your precious Miles."

I recoil from the unfeeling tone. "I mean your father," I shoot back, wanting to hurt him.

He recoils. "Don't you dare talk about my father," he orders.

"No?" I taunt him. Wanting him to hurt, like I do. Wanting him to suffer. "Then how about Bianca's father?" I add. "Or does he not matter to you, either? Just collateral damage along the way."

Sebastian's hand flexes, and for a terrible moment, I wonder what he'll do. What he's capable of, out here in the middle of nowhere, with no rules or audience to hold him back.

Then he narrows his eyes at me. "You should be careful, Little Sparrow," he says, his voice low and deadly. "There's nowhere for you to fly away."

"I was never your Sparrow," I hurl back at him, furious. "You just saw what I wanted you to see. Someone meek, and delicate. Someone you could keep trapped in a gilded cage. God, you were so easy to fool," I say scornfully. Sebastian's jaw clenches tighter, a telltale sign I'm getting to him.

Good.

"Did it make you feel like a big shot, getting to teach the innocent girl?" I continue, taunting him. I know I'm playing with fire here, but I can't hold back. Not anymore. "Did it make you feel like a real man, knowing I had nothing to compare to you? That you were my first, my only one?"

"No." Sebastian growls in answer, his eyes flashing in anger. "It made me feel like a fucking God. The way you would moan for me," he adds, prowling closer to me. "The way you would beg for my cock. *Deeper*," he mimics, "'*God, Seb, more.*' You loved every minute of it. Every fucking inch," he sneers. "And don't think you can deny it now. You may have faked a lot of things, Avery, but even you can't fake the way that sweet cunt went off for me."

"No," I lie, shameful and furious at myself for ever wanting him.

"Yes," he vows, reaching out to grip my chin. He holds me there, his eyes burning into me, rage and something even more dangerous lurking in their depths. "You know it's true. We both do. How much you loved being my good little whore."

I shudder at his words, and we both know, it's not revulsion making my body react.

I wrench away. "I hate you," I vow, shaking with fury.

"Then that's something we have in common, Sparrow. Because I hate me, too."

Sebastian starts walking again, heading determinedly towards the valley.

I have no choice but to follow.

## Chapter 2

### *Avery*

Sebastian sets a fast pace, his longer legs striding through the snow, and it doesn't take me long until I'm out of breath and struggling to keep up. But I refuse to ask him to slow down or admit how much my body is aching.

I'd rather die than show him weakness now.

We walk for hours in silence in the snow, and my muscles are screaming by the time we hit a deserted mountain road. I pause, gasping for breath. "Do you think anyone will be out driving?" I ask hopefully.

He shakes his head. "It's a service road. Emergencies only."

"I'd say this qualifies," I mutter ruefully, as Sebastian checks the compass again, and strides on, still heading north.

No rest for the wicked.

I hoist my bag, and trudge after him. It's easier going now, the road forming a solid surface to walk on, sheltered by the towering fir trees that loom above us, but I'm exhausted, the adrenaline from the crash long since faded, leaving nothing but the icy realization that I don't know what happens next.

If we reach this lodge, if we survive the night…

What will Sebastian do with me then?

As I walk behind him, my face numb from the cold air, I think about what happened back in Italy, how I arranged the lavish party so Sebastian could share our engagement with the world—and instead, I revealed what a monster he truly is. The look of fury and betrayal in his eyes when he finally realized what I'd been planning all this time... The memory of it chills me to the bone, despite the fact that I'm sweating with exertion now.

*Would he hurt me?*

He was planning something, that's for sure. Kidnapping me to a deserted cabin in the mountains? I have to wonder what kind of 'chat' he had in mind, before the plane crash forced him to change his plans. The bitter irony hits hard, that now, after everything, the tables have well and truly turned.

Now *he's* the one out for revenge.

I can't even say I blame him. After all, I single-handedly tore apart everything he'd built—including our twisted charade of a love affair. I spent months scheming to earn his trust, investigating his whole life, while I pretended to fall in love with him.

*Pretended...?*

I feel a desperate ache, deep in my chest. The truth is, the line between love and hate blurred a long time ago. And yes, there was a moment when I thought Sebastian could be redeemed. That his past sins were just that—in the past. That we had the chance to build a future together...

But then he proved me wrong.

The man is heartless. Dangerous.

A monster, just like he always said he was.

Just like I knew, when I set out on this mission to begin with. I was willing to sacrifice my body, my innocence to him, on my quest for vengeance.

But I wasn't expecting to like it.

Because Sebastian was right with his cruel taunting. The sexual connection between us was stronger than any logic or reason. I did crave him. *Beg for him*, as he showed me a pleasure I could never have imagined. I submitted to his every filthy lesson, learning just how far I'd go to win his approval.

That bliss of surrender. The wild release of his low, murmured praise. The words that never failed to make me weak. Make me *wet*.

"*Good girl.*"

I stumble, suddenly overcome with the haunting depths of my failure. I gave up everything to bring Sebastian to justice, I've been torn apart by the war between hatred and desire battling inside of me. I've lied and cheated, and destroyed innocent lives…

And for what?

Sebastian is free. Interpol's handcuffs couldn't hold him for long. And even at the party as I watched them lead him away, I didn't feel triumph, or victory in my apparent success.

Only an emptiness, hollow and aching where my fury had once burned, keeping me warm.

Was it worth it?

Was any of it worth the price I've paid—with my body… and my soul?

My legs give way, and I crumble to my knees into the snow. I feel something inside of me snap. Grief and exhaustion flood through me, and there are suddenly tears stinging my eyes.

*What am I even fighting for anymore?*

"What's the holdup?"

I look up to find Sebastian standing over me with an impatient scowl on his face. "I need to rest," I manage.

"We don't have time to rest." Sebastian snaps. "It'll be dark soon. And a blizzard is coming."

I shake my head weakly, still holding back tears. "I can't."

His jaw tightens. "Avery..."

"I *can't*." My voice breaks, and to my horror, the tears spill over, hot on my cheeks.

Sebastian's icy stare doesn't soften. He just stands there, watching me cry. It's humiliating, to fall apart in front of him, but I can't hold back anymore. My body shakes, and my sobs echo in the stillness of the snow, howling with grief and fear, and everything I've lost on this futile quest for justice, until finally, I'm too drained even to cry.

Sebastian waits, until my sobs become a faint sniffle. "Are you done now?" he says curtly.

I nod, shame red on my face.

"Then start walking."

*Bastard.*

I struggle to my feet again. Sebastian doesn't offer to help, but when I'm finally upright, brushing off the snow, I find him holding out a mini bottle of water from his pack.

I gape. "You had this all along?"

"It's the only one."

I snatch it from him, and gulp it down greedily, forcing myself to stop before I drain the bottle. Reluctantly, I hand it back to him, with a couple of inches of water still left. "You finish it."

Sebastian arches an eyebrow. "How generous," he says dryly. "I'm touched you care."

"Don't flatter yourself," I shoot back. "If you die of thirst, then who's going to lead me to this cabin?"

Sebastian scowls, gulps the water down, and then starts walking again. I hoist my bag and follow.

. . .

Everything is a blur after that. Every step along the deserted mountain road takes a massive effort, and as the afternoon stretches into the evening, the snow begins to fall. It doesn't take long before Sebastian is proven right, and it turns into a blizzard, the flakes whirling around, making it hard to even see twenty feet ahead of us. The sun sets, and the temperature drops even more, chilling me to my core, despite the clammy exertion. Just when I'm wondering if we might actually freeze to death in the dark out here, Sebastian picks up his pace.

"There!" he exclaims, pointing ahead. "Up there!"

I squint through the snow, and just about make out the dark silhouette of a structure, up on the ridge. "The cabin?" I say, my heart leaping with hope.

"We made it." Sebastian confirms, and it's not until I see the relief shining clear in his eyes that I realize, he hasn't been as confident as he's made out.

*We've been in real danger.*

"Thank God," I exhale. The snow whips around us, dizzyingly white, but my energy is renewed, and I manage to struggle up the driveway after him.

As we draw closer, I can make out that it's a rustic lodge, set back near the trees. The door is locked, but that proves no obstacle for Sebastian. He simply hurls himself at it, shoulder-first, and the wood splinters around the lock.

Open.

I stumble inside after him, slamming the door shut behind us against the snow and wind. It's freezing and dark in here, but there's an immediate relief to be out of the blizzard. I catch my breath, stamping the snow off my boots as Sebastian finds a light switch and flips it, but nothing happens.

"Damn it," he curses. "The storm must have knocked out the electricity." He looks out the windows, but we can't see a thing through the dark and whirling snow. "The backup generator is out by the shed; I'll see if I can fix it in the morning."

"What about a phone line?" I ask.

He shakes his head, already lifting the handset on the old-fashioned receiver. "Dead. There's no cell service out here either. The mountains block the signal."

Damn it.

He strips off his outdoor gear and heads deeper into the house, and I can hear him rummaging in a cabinet as I peel off my boots and coat. Then there's a flicker of light, and Sebastian is back, swinging a battery-powered lantern.

"This way," he orders, and I follow him through to the living room. In the light from the lantern, I can see it's a rustic, cozy looking place, full of wood accents and comfy furniture. It's smaller than I would have expected from the great hedge fund billionaire, but right now, I would be happy with a single-room trailer, if there were four walls and a place to sleep.

God, sleep. I'm halfway there already, swaying on my feet as Sebastian goes to the huge stone fireplace that dominates the far wall. He grabs logs from the stack by the wall, and starts to build a fire in the grate, muttering something under his breath as he strikes a match, and lights the old newspaper.

It flares, burning brightly, and I move closer, drawn to the warmth and light. I hold out my frozen, stiff hands, just about ready to collapse.

God, it feels good.

"Get undressed."

I blink at Sebastian in shock. He's looming over me, already pulling off his sweater.

"W-what?" I gape, filled with a rush of telltale desire, despite everything.

*My body still wants him.*

Sebastian unbuttons his shirt, stripping it from his body

with clinical efficiency. "Our clothes are wet through. We need to take them off, otherwise we'll never get warm."

Shirtless, his bare chest glows in the firelight. Taut. Muscular.

*Tempting.*

I avert my gaze, still reluctant. Now that the immediate danger has passed, I'm faced with the more pressing one.

Sebastian and I, alone in the house.

Getting naked.

"I'm fine," I lie, edging closer to the fire. So what if I can barely feel my feet anymore, and I'm shivering so hard my teeth rattle? People take ice plunge baths for fun.

Sebastian exhales a frustrated breath. "Avery, I'm too tired to argue with you anymore. You're cold, and wet through, and the last thing I need is you catching pneumonia while we're stranded out here. So, for the love of God, take off your fucking clothes."

I swallow hard. Even after everything, that steely tone in his voice is impossible to disobey.

"Fine," I mumble, reaching for my damp sweater. "Just don't look."

Sebastian narrows his eyes. "I've already seen it all, Sparrow."

His nickname still makes me shiver, but he's already striding out of the room, leaving me free to strip out of my wet clothing. The warmth of the fire feels incredible against my bare skin, and I practically sigh in pleasure and relief.

Sebastian returns, with a couple of thick, warm bathrobes. "Here," he shoves one at me, then strips off the rest of his clothes, and pulls his own on. We settle on the floor in front of the fire, crowding as close as possible to the flames without getting burned.

Still, my teeth won't stop chattering.

"Do you need anything?" Sebastian's voice comes, gruff.

I shake my head, my arms wrapped around my body, trying to keep my distance from him. "Just warmth," I mutter.

Sebastian curses again under his breath. Then he puts an arm around my shoulders and yanks me closer.

"Hey!" I try to struggle, but Sebastian tucks me in his lap, resting against his chest as if I belong there.

"You can fight me tomorrow," his voice is low in my ear. "Let's just get through tonight, OK?"

I relax. I can't help it. His arms are tight around me, and the warmth from his body seeps into me, just as hot as the fire blazing in the hearth.

God, it feels so good...

I'm so tired that my eyes are already closing, nestled there in Sebastian's embrace. For a moment, I can almost pretend that the past few weeks haven't happened. That we're curled up in bed in London together, back when I wondered if there was a real chance for us. When I saw the softer, vulnerable side to him, and considered loving him for real.

*What I wouldn't give to go back to that moment...*

I yawn, snuggling into him automatically. His arms tighten around me, and I wonder if he's thinking about it, too.

Does he regret what he's done? Does he wish that things could have been different between us?

Or is he sitting there, hating me, planning his revenge?

Then the tiredness takes me over, and I don't wonder about anything at all.

## Chapter 3

### *Avery*

When I finally wake, it feels like I've been asleep for years. I'm curled under the covers in bed, light filtering through the heavy curtains, surrounded by the muffled silence of snow.

Bed...

I look around. I'm lying in a large, comfortable bed in a simply decorated room. Sebastian must have carried me up to a guest suite, sometime in the night.

I pull back the covers, and slowly stand, my body still aching from the hike. Outside the windows, it's daylight, but the sky is cloudy, and snow is still falling thickly, burying any signs of civilization.

The view stretches, powdery and white all the way to the mountains.

I find a bathroom, cringing when I look into the mirror and see my reflection. My hair is a disaster, and I have dark circles under my eyes despite my long sleep. I focus on the cut on my forehead. There's dry blood around it, and I use a wet washcloth to gently clean the area. Sebastian was right, it's not too bad.

My stomach rumbles, reminding me I haven't eaten in days now, so I go in search of food. I gingerly make my way downstairs and take a proper look around. There's the living area we spent last night, with an old piano in the corner, and big vibrant paintings on the wall. Storage… A mudroom with boots and coats… A library nook… I'm just checking the phone line again when a back door opens, and Sebastian walks in, wrapped in a thick coat. He stomps his boots shakes his head, sending snow flying off in every direction.

I tense automatically, preparing myself for more hostilities, but he barely glances in my direction.

"Good news," he says shortly, reaching for the light switch on the wall. He flips it, and the room is bathed in a warm glow. "Generator's back up."

I exhale in relief. "So we have heat and light now?" I ask hopefully.

He nods. "There's coffee in the kitchen," he adds, still curt, before striding off into another room.

Clearly, we're back to the cold treatment, despite the power being back on.

But I'll take it, if he's right about the coffee.

I follow the smell to a small, homey kitchen, with wooden cabinets and ancient looking appliances. I find the coffee waiting in the pot and gulp down a scalding mug before turning my attention to food. The cupboards clearly haven't been stocked in a while, but I find a loaf of sliced bread in the freezer and manage to pry a couple of pieces off to fit in the toaster.

I swear, the few minutes it takes for the bread to thaw feel like hours. I don't even wait to find butter or jam, I just tear pieces off and shove them in my mouth, choking them down with the coffee, in my hurry to eat.

There's noise behind me, and then Sebastian enters. He's dressed casually in jeans and a knit sweater now and moves with careful precision around the small space: pouring his coffee into a mug, adding creamer, and then making two slices of toast with butter and honey from the cupboard.

He doesn't look at me once, not even when he finally takes a seat, and starts eating his breakfast like he's dining at a five-star restaurant.

I get it. I'm the ravenous animal, eating with my bare hands.

"The snow's still coming down," he says, finally acknowledging my presence. "We'll likely be trapped here a few days."

"Great." I mumble, grabbing some of that honey, and smearing it on the bread. I don't care if I look like a ravenous beast right now, swear, I've never been so hungry in my life before.

"Luckily, I keep my stores well stocked." Sebastian watches me eat, with something like disdain on his infuriatingly handsome face. "There should be supplies in the cellar. When you're done here, you can make yourself useful and take inventory, before you eat us out of house and home."

His tone is clipped and patronizing. Clearly, our ceasefire from last night is over, and he's back to hating my very being. I'm the last person in the world he wants to be snowed in with.

And the feeling is mutual.

I match his cool stare with one of my own. "Fine," I say, icy. "Anything else?"

His scowl deepens. "You could try putting some damn clothes on."

I glance down. My robe has fallen open at the neck, revealing my bare cleavage. "Is that a problem for you?" I coo, toying with the neckline, parting it a little wider, just to get a rise out of him. "Like you said, it's nothing you haven't seen before."

Sebastian just scowls and walks out.

Fine. I yank the belt tighter, and finish eating before going to follow his orders. *Orders*. As if he has any right to boss me around, after everything that's happened. If he hadn't come after me on the plane, then we wouldn't be stranded out here.

Hell, maybe the plane wouldn't have crashed at all without him masquerading as the pilot.

I grab my bag, and haul it upstairs, where I find some women's clothing in the guest room closet and dresser. I shouldn't be surprised, but I can't help feeling a stab of jealousy as I turn on the hot water, filling the small bathroom with delicious steam.

Which is crazy. Sebastian and I are over, I remind myself sternly. Even our pretense at affection is dead; there's no act to get swept up in anymore. No more faked emotion to blur the lines to the real thing.

It should be a relief. Instead, it feels like a loss.

I take my sweet time getting cleaned up, letting the hot water run over my bruised, aching body. Nothing can wash away the stress and terror of the past twenty-four hours, but I try, and by the time I emerge, scrubbed clean, I feel refreshed and ready to face my next challenge. After all, I survived a plane crash and a grueling hike through the wilderness. I can deal with a day or two under the same roof as Sebastian. Especially now that there's heating and hot water.

I continue my pep talk as I dress in some of the underwear I grabbed from my case, and a borrowed sweater and jeans. Soon enough, the snow will stop, and we'll be able to call for rescue. Until then, I'll just have to grit my teeth and make it through as best I can.

Starting with figuring out our food situation.

I decide to do as Sebastian suggested and check out the cabin's stocks. He was an asshole about it, but I do want to know how long we can survive out here.

The last thing we need is to run out of food.

There's no sign of Sebastian when I come back downstairs, so I get organized, finding a notepad and pen, and methodically going through every cupboard in the kitchen. There's almost nothing there, it's clear nobody's been at the cabin for months, but just when I'm starting to worry, I go down to the cellar like he suggested, and hit paydirt. A fully stocked pantry of canned and dry goods, plus a freezer chest full of meat and frozen bread. I'm guessing that even though the power went out, it was too cold here for anything to thaw, so it'll be safe enough to eat. We have enough to last weeks if necessary.

*Weeks...* I feel a chill at the thought, despite the cozy temperature inside. Being trapped with Sebastian that long, I don't know if I would kill the man.

Or even worse, kiss him.

I block out the thought and focus on staying busy instead. I grab a box, and load up some provisions from the cellar stores, bringing them up to the kitchen. I'm just unpacking them when a movement outside the window catches my eye. I see Sebastian emerge from the small woodshed with a pile of thick logs in his arms. He's wearing a coat, but it's unbuttoned, allowing me to see his gray T-shirt stretched across his broad chest. His jaw is set, and I know that the load he's carrying must be heavy.

I know the strength coiled in that taut physique.

*His hands gripping tightly on my hips... His weight pinning me to the mattress...*

*His cock driving deep inside of me, hitting just the perfect spot...*

An aching heat blooms deep inside me, and I have to force myself to look away. The usual wash of shame follows the desire, and God, I'm sick of being torn between loathing and lust like this. I don't want to feel this way about him anymore. This sexual connection between us may be thrilling and terrifying, but it has brought me nothing but trouble.

*When will I be free of him?*

Soon, I vow. Soon, this will be over. Despite my despair yesterday, I have more clarity now. He may have ducked out of custody, but Sebastian's a wanted man, completely ruined in the eyes of the public. When the blizzard passes and we can get out of here, I'll go home and hopefully, he'll go to prison. Or maybe into hiding. It doesn't matter. All I care about is that I've destroyed the life he had, taken the wealth, and status he loved so much, and burned them all to ashes, the way I promised to avenge Miles' death.

And I'll never have to see him again.


I spend the rest of the day holed up in the tiny library I found, tucked in the back of the house. The walls are lined with bookcases, and there's a comfy chair by a fireplace. I settle in with a book, relishing the chance to escape reality for a few hours.

Sebastian leaves me alone in blissful solitude, lost in a thick fantasy novel, and I'm not even sure how much time has passed when I'm pulled back to reality by delicious food smells wafting from the kitchen.

My stomach lets out a growl.

I put my book down and stand, stretching out my stiff body after hours of immobility. I have no idea what's cooking, but it smells too good to resist, so I make my way to the kitchen. I find Sebastian there, making dinner. He's chopping vegetables and has a big pot of something bubbling on the stove, sending up that hearty scent.

I watch him a moment from the doorway. It's crazy how

moments like this, he seems like a different person: unguarded, even relaxed.

Then he looks up, and his whole body tightens with tension again. There's a moment of silence as our eyes meet, the tension thick enough to cut with one of those deadly looking knives he's using to slice bread.

"Smells good," I offer blandly. He doesn't reply. Instead, he ladles stew into a bowl, and goes to sit at the table. He starts eating, alone, as if I'm not even here.

I scowl.

So, I guess he wants me to ask nicely, despite all the resentment and bad blood between us. Hell, that's probably *why* he's waiting for me to ask. It's a power trip.

Everything is like that with him.

I'm in no mood for any more of his games, but the stew looks amazing, so I take a deep breath, and ask as pleasantly as I can, "Is there enough for two?"

"Would you like some?" His smirk makes me feel violent. I bite back a bitter retort.

"Yes, I would. Thank you."

"Go ahead," he finally nods to the pot, and I rush to fill a bowl and join him at the table.

Damn, it's good.

The rich flavors of the stew are heaven, and the way the warmth of it soothes me from the inside out is exactly what I needed. Despite the tension still shimmering in the air between us, I find myself relaxing back into my chair, and I can't help asking Sebastian the question that's been on my mind.

"These clothes..." I ask slowly. "Who do they belong to?"

He doesn't answer right away, and I watch as he dips a piece of bread in his stew and tears off a chunk with his teeth. His every movement is deliberate, just like everything else he does, and I can't help noticing how neat he is. Not a drop of soup spilled. His napkin always at the ready. He's meticulous.

*The way he was attending to my body.*

"They belong to Scarlett," he finally says, and I focus back on the conversation. "I bring her here sometimes."

His sister. That makes sense.

I tell myself that I wasn't feeling jealous, but there's no denying the relief I feel at his explanation. Since we're talking now, I decide to ask the other question that's been weighing heavily on my mind.

"What do you think will happen, when they realize we're gone, and they can't find the plane?"

Sebastian curls his lip in a hollow smirk. "They'll assume we're dead."

"Oh."

I suspected as much, but it's different to hear him say the words. I think of the people I love, and I hate knowing that they'll assume the worst. *Nero, Lily…* With any luck, I'll be able to call in a few days and let them know I'm OK, but still, a few days is a long time to grieve.

But I guess there's no choice about it now.

"It's what you wanted, isn't it?" Sebastian asks, and I have to take a moment to follow what he's saying. "Me, dead," he continues, a dark look in his eyes.

"Not dead," I reply quietly. "Just you wishing that you were."

He snorts, bitter. "My mistake."

"You asked," I reply with a shrug. In a way, it's a relief, not to have to lie and pretend anymore. My old resentment is out in the open now, I don't need to act sweet and innocent anymore. "So yes, that was my mission. I set out to find the one thing you loved more than anything and take it from you."

Sebastian meets my eyes, burning and intense. "Well, you

did it," he replies simply. "Congratulations. Mission accomplished."

He pushes back his chair, before I can ask what he means. He rinses his bowl, and then walks out of the room, leaving me with the question whirling in my mind.

What did he love more than anything?

His wealth? His power?

Or... *Me?*

I finish my meal, and wander through to the living room, needing something to occupy me for the evening—so I don't go down that dangerous path wondering what Sebastian meant.

I find myself drawn to the piano, taking a seat on the bench. I haven't played in a while, with everything that's been going on, but just like usual, all it takes it me resting my fingers on the keys to feel suddenly centered again. More like myself.

You can't lie to an instrument. There's no betraying wood and ivory.

Taking a deep breath, I start playing without even thinking about it. The first notes of "Both Sides Now" fill the air and it's not long before I'm softly singing the words, letting myself wallow in the melancholy emotions that wash over me. The music sweeps me away, and as the final notes ring out, I open my eyes again. Somehow, I'm not surprised to find Sebastian watching me, leaning in the doorway, his expression inscrutable.

I feel that ache in my chest again.

This isn't the first time he's watched me singing at the piano. I remember the first time, when we'd only just met. I was sure of everything back then. I had a plan.

Now, I know there's no planning when it comes to this man. No logic, or rational thought.

And I can tell, he feels the same.

"What was that song?" he asks quietly.

"Joni Mitchell." I reply. "It's about how you can never really know what love means."

"Romantic." Sebastian's lip curls, sarcastic, but I shrug.

"I think it is. Knowing that the one you love can hurt you but loving them all the same."

It's not until the words leave my mouth that I realize I could be describing the two of us. I look away, blushing, but Sebastian slowly moves closer, until he's standing at my side. He rests a hand on my shoulder, sweeping my hair back, and I tense.

He pauses. "Are you scared of me?"

I glance up at him and feel the spike of adrenalin kick through my veins. "Yes," I admit, even though the truth isn't quite so simple.

I'm not just scared of him, but what I'll do with him. Even now, after everything, the touch of his hand on my body makes me ache.

*Wanting more.*

Sebastian arches an eyebrow, still looking down at me, where I'm seated on the piano stool. "Funny. I should be the one who's scared. You schemed and planned my destruction. You fooled me."

Is that pain I see in his eyes? Or just hatred and desire?

"You deserved it." I reply.

Sebastian gives a bitter laugh at that. "Yes, I did. And you came to make me pay for my sins. An angel of justice."

"Or the devil you've been running from," I reply.

His lips twist in a sad, aching smile. "Maybe we died in the crash, after all," he muses, his voice almost a whisper. His hand trails over my shoulder again, caressing the bare slope of my neck, making me shiver. "To be stuck here with you, in this torment... Hating you. Wanting you. Maybe this really is hell."

*Yes.*

Relief crashes through me, that he understands exactly how I feel.

Relief—and desire.

Sebastian yanks me closer, and then his lips are on mine in a cold, punishing kiss. I moan against him to feel his mouth again, heat racing through my body as his hands grip my shoulders, and his tongue plunges deep, commanding me. Devouring me.

This is the madness I've been craving. The insanity that pulls me under in an instant, with no regard for the truth.

I arch up, eager to lose myself in him again. But too soon, he pulls away, leaving me gasping.

"Keep playing," he orders me.

I swallow, my head spinning.

"Play for me," he insists, moving to stand behind me, his hands resting on my shoulders. "When you play... I can forgive you almost anything."

I inhale in a rush. I don't know what's happening here, but the lust is beating through me, thick in my bloodstream. That dark, familiar sweetness that blots out all reason, and urges me to cross the line.

Slowly, I move my hands back to the keys, and begin to play. It's a simple melody, but simple is all I can manage when Sebastian slowly starts to strip me where I sit.

First my sweater, then my slip. He tugs them up, over my head, and I barely break my playing long enough to lift my arms in turn and allow him to lift the fabric free.

The cool air brings goosebumps along my arms. Or maybe that's just from Sebastian's slow caress, trailing his fingertips over my now-bare skin, making my breath hitch, and my blood run hotter.

He unhooks my bra behind me and lets the silk fall free to my waist.

I shiver, struggling to focus on my playing. I'm bared to him now. Painfully aware of his hands, still skimming over my shoulders... My collarbone...

My bare breasts.

I gasp as his hands cup me from behind.

"Don't stop." Sebastian's voice is a growl in my ear. An order.

And God, I love to obey his instructions.

I keep playing, my hands shaking as he slowly squeezes and fondles my breasts. His thumb and forefingers close around one stiff nipple, pinching almost painfully, but oh, the sensation spirals straight to my core. I'm gasping, thighs clenching, by the time his hand moves back up to grip my jaw.

He sinks his thumb between my lips, and I suck.

*Fuck.*

He groans, low and throaty, and the sound only makes me hotter. *Wetter.* I'm shaking now under his slow, deliberate touch, every nerve ending in my body alert and screaming for more. *Desperate.*

My hands fumble. My head is cloudy. "Seb..." I whisper, half-moaning as I try to turn to look at him. But Sebastian forces my head to stay facing forwards.

"No," he growls. "I can't look at you." He hauls me up, bending me painfully over the piano keys, so I'm facedown with my cheek pressed to the scuffed wood. "I can't watch you lie anymore."

Sebastian's breath comes faster; he's panting as I hear the snap of his belt, and the sound of his pants being yanked down. "But your body can't lie, can it?" he demands, running a possessive hand over my bare back. He unfastens my jeans, and tugs them down over my hips, landing a stinging slap on my bare ass. "This tight cunt always tells me the truth. Doesn't it?"

I gasp for air, my head spinning. My body is aching, and

I'm already spreading my legs wider, arching eagerly back towards him.

"Doesn't it?" Sebastian demands again, with another sharp spank. His fingers rove between my legs, dipping into my wetness, rubbing possessively like my pussy belongs to him.

It does.

"Yes!" I cry, loving the feel of his palm against my bare skin. I wriggle my ass, already clenching for what I know is coming. "Yes, please Seb. *Please…*"

"That's right, darling. Beg for daddy."

I don't even have a chance to brace myself before he slams his cock inside me, burying himself deep with one punishing stroke.

*Fuck!*

I let out a loud scream of shock and pleasure as he thrust deeper, relentless, fucking me all the way to the hilt.

"Goddamn, Avery," he groans, sounding ragged. "*Fuck.*"

He grinds up, embedded deep inside me, fucking me up onto my tiptoes as I gasp for air. But there's no escaping it, he's got both my arms pinned behind my back to hold me in place, yanking my body back to take his cock even deeper, riding me like a wild beast.

*God.*

I sob, writhing in his arms. It's too deep, too much, but Sebastian doesn't pause for breath. He pulls back, and then slams into me again, over and over, taking his pleasure without reprieve in a merciless rhythm that leaves me screaming. It's rough, and raw, and *fuck*, I can't get enough. Already, the pleasure is spiraling tighter, deep inside me. Already, I'm thrusting back with every harsh stroke, wanting more.

Needing it to hurt. The way I deserve.

"Seb…" I sob, writhing and clawing in his arms as his cock pounds into me, thick and relentless. "Seb!"

"That's right," he groans, slamming into me again, sending my body jolting with the force of impact. "You can't lie to me like this, not when you're too busy screaming my fucking name!"

*Oh God. It's too good. Too sweet. Too much to take.*

"Maybe I'll keep you like this," Sebastian's voice is harsh and ragged, his body pinning me to the piano, owning me from the inside out. "Chain you to the bed with your legs spread for me, Little Sparrow. Keep you fucked and full all day long, so you can't betray me anymore. You'd like that, wouldn't you?"

I sob, so close to the edge I can't bear it. Can't even pretend his words don't fill me with a filthy fire. *To be at his mercy...*

I shudder at the idea, and Sebastian gives a cruel laugh, feeling the way my pussy clenches around him. "I wouldn't even need the chains, would I?" he taunts, sliding a hand between my thighs to rub at my swollen clit as he slams into me again. "We both know, you'll be a good girl and take it anywhere I like. This pussy... Your sweet mouth..." Sebastian leans down, so his voice is raw in my ear. "That tight, virgin ass."

*Fuck.*

The shock and pleasure of his filthy promise is too much to take. My climax bursts through me like an avalanche, sending me spiraling with a scream. Sebastian slams into me again, once, twice, and then comes with a roar, shuddering as he unleashes his own climax deep inside me.

I'm still reeling, collapsed over the piano, when he releases me. I manage to lift my head, glancing back at him as he yanks his pants up again. Our eyes meet, and it's like looking in a mirror. Every ounce of shame and self-loathing I feel is echoed in Sebastian's gaze.

He hates himself for wanting me, too.

"This changes nothing, you know," I say coolly, forcing

myself to straighten. I make a show of stretching, displaying my naked body to him, still breathless with pleasure that I try to hide. "Just because we fuck, it doesn't mean I forgive you for anything."

Sebastian sneers at me. "I wasn't asking for your forgiveness, Sparrow. And in case you've forgotten, I'm not the only one who's sinned."

"You're really comparing our crimes?" I ask in disbelief, hating the guilt I feel over my own transgressions. "Because I'm not the one with blood on my hands."

"No, you're the one with my cum dripping out of you," he says crudely, and I gasp in shock.

"Fuck you," I scowl, grabbing at my clothes.

"I already did," he shoots back, coldly zipping up his fly again. "And we both know it's not the last time, either. Face it, Little Sparrow, we're trapped here together with nothing to do but fight and fuck. And the sooner you admit you love it that way, the sooner I'll give you what you've really been craving."

"And what's that?" I ask angrily, already striding for the stairs.

His eyes drift over me as I pass him. His lips curl in smug triumph.

"My praise."

# Chapter 4

## *Avery*

As much as I hate to admit it, Sebastian is right. That night over the piano wasn't the last time we have sex. Not even close.

For the next few days, we settle into a tense, furious routine. By day, we keep our distance, busying ourselves with projects around the cabin. Sebastian tends to the generator and electrical system, spending hours out back in the yard, chopping wood, while I lock myself up in the library, and try to lose myself in the thick novels lining the walls.

It doesn't work. Every hour in this place is just a silent countdown, to when we finish dinner, and put the last of the dishes aside, and then Sebastian wordlessly climbs the staircase to his bedroom.

And I obediently follow after him.

I hate myself for it, but I want him even more. There's nothing in the world like it, the way he takes over me, the moment we step inside the bedroom, chasing every other thought away with his cool instructions and unbreakable will. Dominating me the way nobody else ever has.

The way I never knew I always needed.

Yes, Sebastian still has an unshakeable hold over me. Part desire, part obsession. *All mine.*

I wish those nights would last forever. The sharp ache of pleasure he conjures with his hands, his tongue, his thick, relentless cock. The way he knows exactly how to strip away all my defenses, leaving me writhing, begging for just another taste, soaring with the thrill of total surrender.

The wild, ravenous look in his eyes as I sink to my knees, open my mouth, and suck him all the way down.

"Fuck, Avery, just like that…"

"Deeper, baby, take it all."

*"Good girl."*

It's heaven. I can't get enough. I revel in it, blissfully free—until I wake alone in my own bed the next morning, and it all comes rushing back to me. My shame. My anger.

Sebastian's wicked heart.


The snow finally stops falling on the third day. I settle into the library as usual to pass the day, but I'm interrupted when Sebastian comes into the study for the first time since I claimed it as my own. He's dressed in his coat and boots, holding a rifle.

"I'm going hunting."

My eyebrows pop up. "Clearly," I say, cautiously eying the gun.

"Are you coming?" he asks.

I'm already on my feet. I'm so restless from being cooped up in here, I'd do anything to get out—even venture into the snow with an armed man who hates me. "Give me five minutes," I tell him, quickly going to change into warm clothes. I layer up with boots and a coat from the mudroom, and meet Sebastian in the backyard, which is thickly covered in snow.

"There should be deer in the forest," he says, nodding to where the tree line begins in the distance.

"We're hunting Bambi?" I protest.

He gives me a look. "What do you think you've been eating for days?"

"I've been trying not to think about it at all," I admit.

"Come on. Be quiet," he adds, adjusting his pack. "And stay near me. The lake's frozen, but the ice isn't safe."

I pull my mittens on and set off after him. The sky is clear, bright and crisp, and the snow lays thickly on the ground, totally undisturbed. I take a deep breath, savoring the chilled air in my lungs. It's beautiful out here—or, it would be, if this were some romantic getaway, and not the two of us stranded together, bound by necessity and loathing.

Still, the change of scene is exactly what I needed, and I'm enjoying the nature as we trek along the edge of the forest, the fir trees looming thickly all around. Then I feel Sebastian's hand on my arm.

"This way," he says, nodding deeper into the forest.

"Aren't we walking on a trail right now? Maybe we shouldn't leave it," I suggest. "We don't want to get lost."

Sebastian shakes his head. "We need to hunt in the cross wind."

My eyebrows knit together as I stare at him in confusion.

"The wind needs to blow from the side as we walk," he explains. "Deer have sensitive noses and if they catch our scent, they'll avoid us."

"You really think we'll find any deer?"

"Only if you be quiet," he says, looking annoyed.

I glare at him but don't say another word as I make an effort move as silently as possible. Luckily, the snow help stifle the sound of us walking as we step off the path. Sebastian moves stealthily through the trees, and I try to mimic that, following a few steps behind.

Sebastian suddenly stops walking and holds up a hand. I pause, watching him. But his gaze is trained on something in front of him through the trees. It's a deer, head bent, sniffing in the undergrowth.

I freeze, hardly daring to breathe. The deer hasn't noticed us yet, but I know enough to be sure that he'll run away quickly if he senses us.

"Here," Sebastian whispers, moving closer to me. I shiver, and it has nothing to do with the cold. "You take the shot."

He hands over the gun, surprising me. With all the mistrust lingering between us, I wasn't expecting him to give me a weapon.

It's heavy in my hands. I shift my feet to shoulder-width apart to steady my stance as I bring the rifle up, putting the butt of it against my shoulder as I aim it in the direction of where the deer is standing. My trigger hand is on the handgrip and the other grips the stock.

"You've done this before," Sebastian whispers, and I realize he's moved behind me. But he's so close, I can feel his warm breath on the back of my neck.

"I've fired a rifle," I admit quietly, lowering my head until my cheek rests against the butt of the rifle, my line of sight directly through the scope. "My dad took me to the shooting range a couple of times when I was a teenager," I add. "I learned how to shoot there with him. It was one of our rare bonding experiences."

Skills I'd need in the Barretti world.

Sebastian reaches around and adjusts my aim. "Aim for the area behind the shoulder. You want a clean kill, so it doesn't suffer."

I'm surprised he would even care, but I do as he says, aiming carefully, my finger on the trigger. One... two... three—

I hesitate for a split-second, not sure I want to follow through. That's all it takes. The deer startles, suddenly racing away into the forest.

I lower the rifle. "Sorry," I say, but when I turn, Sebastian is watching me, looking puzzled.

"Why didn't you take the shot?"

I shrug. "It's a harmless animal. What gives us the right to take its life?"

He arches an eyebrow. "You pretend to have morals. How sweet."

"And you pretend like you don't," I shoot back. "That's what I don't understand about you, Sebastian. One minute, you act like you're a heartless monster, and the next, you're funding orphanages, and trying to make amends for your crimes. Which is it? I get whiplash trying to keep up!"

"Which do you think it is?" he demands, grabbing my arm and yanking me closer to him. His eyes are blazing urgently, the tension rippling with every word. "Tell me, Avery," he orders me. "Which side of the scales do my sins fall?"

"I... don't know," I reply, helplessly staring back at him. The heat shimmers between us, his face just inches from mine.

With a groan, Sebastian kisses me.

*Yes.*

I fall into the embrace, my heart pounding in my chest. It doesn't matter that we're wearing bulky coats. Just being this close to him makes my blood run hot in my veins, nothing but the silence of the forest around us, and my own racing desire, urging me on.

Sebastian curses against my mouth, then he's pulling back, and reaching for his pants.

"On your knees, baby," he commands me, freeing his cock.

His breath is ragged, but the look in his eyes is pure steel as he leans back against a tree and fixes me with a dominating look. "Open wide and give me that sweet mouth."

I'm the one with a loaded gun in my hands, but we both know, that means nothing. In an instant, he effortlessly takes control.

And I willingly give it to him.

I sink to the snow without a word of protest, already shivering with excitement. He's hard, thick and demanding, and I part my lips obediently, rocked back there on my heels as Sebastian slowly presses his straining cock into my mouth with a hiss of satisfaction.

"That's it," he groans, as I swirl my tongue over his head. "Fuck, that's perfect. You know what I need."

And I do.

The flush of awareness spreads through me, glowing hotter as I angle my head, and take him deeper, almost to the back of my throat. Sebastian's hands tangle in my hair, urging me on, and I lose myself in the thrust of his thick flesh, and his groans of satisfaction, and my own answering moans, humming deep as I work him with my lips, and tongue, losing myself in the rush of it all. The freedom of total surrender that only he can give.

"That's my girl," he groans, thrusting faster now, fucking my mouth without mercy. "That's my good fucking girl."

I moan in answer, dizzy with lust, and I can't resist slipping a hand between my own legs, rubbing myself through the fabric of my jeans as I choke around his cock. It's not enough, not nearly good enough, but somehow the sharp friction and Sebastian's wild thrusts send me higher, higher, until I'm sobbing with need for my own release, so close to—

"Stop."

Sebastian growls the order, and my hand freezes, even as

my body aches. He pulls out of my mouth with a wet pop, tilting my head up to him. "You don't come unless I say you can," he says clearly, eyes burning into mine. "Don't forget for one minute, your pleasure belongs to me, and always will."

I gasp there, on my knees in the snow, so close to release. I can't believe it, but his denial somehow brings me even closer to the edge. Only he has this power over me.

Only he could make it this sweet.

"Look at you, such a needy girl..." Sebastian croons softly, caressing my cheek. "Do you want to come?"

I nod eagerly. "Please," I gasp. "I'm so close..."

"Then earn it," he replies, with a triumphant smile, fisting his thick cock in his other hand. "Get back to work, baby. And swallow every drop."

I don't hesitate. I lunge for his cock, taking him deep into my mouth with renewed vigor. Sebastian's desperate groans drive me on, intoxicating, as I lap and suck, giving myself over to his pleasure, chasing his every gasp and cry until he's gripping my hair tightly, thrusting with wild abandon. I'm choking on his girth, but I don't care. All that matters is the way his cock leaps in my mouth, the telltale sign that he's close.

That he's mine.

I swallow him down, massaging him with the walls of my throat in a secret embrace. "Fuck," Sebastian cries out, suddenly exploding in a rush of hot liquid, flooding my mouth. "Goddamn. *Avery*..."

His howl of pleasure echoes through the forest, mingling with the sound of my own racing heart as he thrusts into my willing mouth, over and over, riding his climax to the end.

Still, I don't pause, or break for air. No, I do exactly as he says.

I swallow every drop.

"Good girl," he groans, ragged and gasping. "Now you can come for me."

*Yes.*

It doesn't take much to get me there. Just a couple of presses against the seam of my jeans, and I'm falling into my orgasm, shuddering, lost to the pleasure of it all.

When he finally pulls free, I'm gasping. Sebastian collapses back against the tree, and drags a hand through his hair, looking down at me with an unreadable expression on his face.

"What?" I ask, unsteadily getting to my feet.

"I don't know you at all." Sebastian's answer is simple, but somehow chills me. A reminder of the roles I've been playing with him since the very first day, and all our cruel games.

"Yes, you do," I reply, turning away from him, and brushing snow from my knees.

"I know how to get you off," Sebastian corrects me, hoisting the rifle from where I left it. "That's nothing."

I bridle. Somehow hearing him say it like that, so dismissively, makes me feel cheap, after everything we just did. Reminding me, it means nothing to him. Just a way to pass the time while we're stranded here. A sign of his power over me, nothing more, nothing less.

"That's rich, coming from the king of emotional unavailability," I reply, starting to walk back in the direction we came.

Sebastian follows. "Unavailable?" he gives a harsh laugh. "Avery, I opened my life to you. I was an open fucking book. But then, you planned it that way, didn't you?" he demands, drawing level. "Setting your traps, baiting the hook, just waiting for me to step into range to take your shot... You might have spared that deer, but you're plenty ruthless when it comes to your prey."

"Says the man who kidnapped me!" I yell back at him. "Look around, Sebastian. Who's the ruthless one now? If you hadn't hijacked the plane, we would never have crashed here!"

Sebastian looks at me like I'm crazy. "You think that was my fault?"

"I don't see anyone else here," I retort, stomping through the snow.

"You might have been too distracted to notice the state of the plane when we crashed, but I saw the wreckage." Sebastian says, curt. "The plane went down because of a deliberate explosion."

I stop dead in disbelief. "You mean... a bomb?"

"Yes." There's no hesitation. I can see it in his eyes, it's the truth.

*Oh my God.*

I reel back, stunned. "Someone tried to kill you..."

My mind races to who could have done it, but there's no shortage of suspects. And I can tell, Sebastian is thinking the same thing. After my very public unmasking of him, there's at least a dozen people who would love to take their shot to wipe Sebastian Wolfe from the face of the earth.

And end my life in the process.

"Avery..." he takes a step towards me, but I recoil, shaken.

"No!" I cry. "Don't touch me." I back away from him. "I can't believe this, I nearly died because of you. But you don't care, do you? We're all just collateral damage along the way."

I turn and run, as fast as I can in the snow. Emerging from the forest, I see the dark silhouette of the cabin across the snowy expanse and cut in that direction.

"Avery!" Sebastian's voice calls behind me. "Avery, stop!"

I keep running, but I stumble in the snow, as Sebastian races after me "Avery, stop!" he yells. "The ice! It's not safe!"

I freeze, looking wildly around.

Ice?

I remember too late what he said, that beneath all this snow is a lake. Frozen over for winter. But how thickly?

"What do I do?" I call, panicking.

"Don't move!" Sebastian yells back. He comes to a stop twenty feet away from me, looking wildly around.

I automatically start moving towards him. "Sebastian…"

A faint cracking begins to sound. Sebastian's eyes widen. "Don't. Move." He barks out.

I stand in place, terrified.

"Just stay right there." He takes a cautious step towards me, then another. The cracking sound echoes. Our eyes meet, and I see the worry in his gaze.

"Seb—"

Before I can even finish, there's another loud CRACK. The ice beneath him gives way, and Sebastian plunges into the icy lake.

# Chapter 5

## *Avery*

"Sebastian!" I scream, watching in disbelief as he disappears, sinking into the lake.

I rush forward, panic overriding my caution about the splintering ice. I reach the edge of the shattered ice in time to see him go under, his hands clawing at the edges to try and grab a solid hold. But he can't, the ice is too sharp, and in his thick coat and hunting gear, he's weighed down, pulled under the surface.

I stand there, dazed for a moment, watching him sink beneath the icy water.

Going... Going...

Gone.

The water closes over him, like he was never even here at all. Sebastian Wolfe, disappeared from this earth, leaving barely a ripple behind.

*No.*

I'm shocked back to action. I look around desperately. I don't know what to do. I don't know how to help him without falling through myself.

*Think.*

I back up, turning and racing to the edge of the lake, looking around for something, anything to help me at all. I grab a thick, fallen tree branch, and then drag it back, carefully edging closer to the opening, then crawling, trying to spread my weight and not put any more pressure on the ice. I lie there and hold the branch out into the water.

"Sebastian!" I scream, searching the dark depths of the lake. "Sebastian!"

He surfaces, gasping and coughing for air.

Relief slams through me. *Oh, thank God.*

"Grab hold of the branch," I yell, holding it out to Sebastian as he struggles to stay above the surface. His eyes are unfocused, and his movements are sluggish now. I can see that the sub-zero temperatures are sending his body into shock. "Sebastian!" I scream louder, trying to break through his daze. "Take the branch!"

He finally does, clumsily grabbing hold of it. Gritting my teeth, I pull with all of my strength, hauling him closer, until he manages to lever himself up, halfway onto the ice. I grab his arm, and yank him the rest of the way, until he finally falls to the ground beside me, panting hard.

"You're frozen," I gulp, panicking. His skin is practically translucent, and his whole body is shaking violently. Whatever cold we experienced on the hike over here, it's nothing compared to this. "We have to get you home."

"In a minute..." he mutters faintly, not moving.

My panic grows. "No. *Now.*"

Still, he doesn't move. I wrack my brain for a way to break through his stupor. Then I remember, how I was in shock after the plane crash and Sebastian snapped me out of it.

CRACK.

I slap him hard across the face.

Sebastian's eyes fly open, and thank God, they're more focused this time. "What...?" he mumbles.

"Lean on me," I order him, struggling to haul him to his feet. Despite his murmured protests, Sebastian doesn't struggle this time. There's ice on his eyelashes, and his breath is rasping. *Fuck.* "Come on, Sebastian," I plead, almost buckling under his soaked weight. "We just need to get you warm. Won't that be nice?" I say, encouraging. "A hot fire, and a bath. You'll be just fine."

"Warm..." he echoes, still wracked with shakes.

I swallow back a sob and steer us to the cabin. He stumbles beside me, almost falling a dozen times before we make it back inside. I steer him straight through to the fire, dropping him to the floor in front of it as I fumble to add several logs and strike a match.

My hands shake. The light won't catch.

"Please," I mutter, desperate. "Please light."

Finally, the match strikes, and I touch it to the newspaper in the grate. The fire flares to life. I turn back to Sebastian, who's lolling there, looking dazed. "Let's get you out of these clothes," I say, masking my panic with a bright tone.

He doesn't protest, as I strip him naked, his limbs heavy and weak. I grab a thick wool blanket from the back of the couch and throw it over his shoulders.

"Stay here. I'll be right back."

I don't know what I'm looking for as I rush into the downstairs bathroom, but I rummage through the cabinets anyway. All I find is an old first aid kit, but there's nothing useful inside, just some old bandages and iodine.

*Damn it.*

I hurry up the stairs to Sebastian's room, grabbing the thickest sweatpants and clothing I can find. When I get back to the living room, I find Sebastian where I left him, huddled under the blanket with his gaze on the fire. He's still shivering, and his eyelids look heavy, as if he might pass out.

"Here, let's get you dressed," I say, kneeling in front of him to pull on his socks. I figure it's a good idea to start with warming up his extremities.

"I've got it," he says, but he doesn't move. As if even dressing himself is too much effort right now. I quickly get him dressed, and then go fix some soup. I spoon-feed it to him right there in front of the fire, but he won't take more than a few mouthfuls of the broth before slumping back, shaking his head.

"Tired," he whispers. "Need rest."

"Sebastian..." My heart is in my throat, watching him shiver. I wish there was more that I could do.

I take his hands in mine, trying to warm them. Trying to hold onto something to stop myself spiraling out with panic and despair.

Sebastian takes a rasping breath and looks at me, his eyes slipping back into focus for a moment. "My sparrow..." He whispers, squeezing my hand softly. Then he lays back, his voice so faint I barely hear his next words under the crack and hiss of the fire:

"*I'm sorry...*"

I don't sleep. I'm too worried about Sebastian to rest, even for a moment. I spend the night by the fire with him, anxiously checking his temperature, and trying to remember anything I might have learned about treating exposure or hypothermia.

Am I supposed to keep him hot? Or cool? Does he need to eat, or is it better to let him sleep straight through, and let his body recover from the shock of the ice?

I wish I knew for sure or had a cell signal to check online. All I can do is press a damp cloth to his forehead and press a cup of water to his lips every few hours, as Sebastian mumbles in his sleep.

"Avery..."

I sit up, startled. It's still dark out, but the fire has burned low in the hearth. I must have drifted off.

"Avery... No!" Sebastian's voice echoes in the dim room, and I spring to my feet.

"Sebastian?" I go to him, but he's still sleeping, thrashing restlessly where he lays by the fire.

"You can't—don't... Don't!"

"Shh," I try to comfort him. "Sebastian, it's OK, I'm right here."

Still, he mumbles, and breaks into a rasping cough, gasping for air. His whole body wracked with the effort.

*Fuck.*

This isn't good. I press a hand to check his forehead, then pull it back, shocked. He's burning up. "I'm going to get you more water," I tell him, but Sebastian grabs my arm.

"No... No," he pulls me closer. "Don' leave... Avery..."

I try to break his hold. "You need to drink."

"Don't go..." he whispers, pulling me closer. "Don't ever go..."

He's out of it, still half-conscious, but his grip is still like steel as yanks me into the curve of his body.

I have no choice but to lay there, spooned against him. His body pressed against me, his mouth tucked against my neck.

Even after everything, even with fear still beating in my chest for him, I can't deny how right it feels to be back in his arms.

Like I belong here.

Sebastian must feel the same, because he exhales, his arms tightening around me. Something in him seems to settle, soothed by my nearness, and our familiar embrace. I don't have the heart to pull away, not with his breathing turning more even, and his restlessness stilled.

I shouldn't want peace for him. But here I am, wishing it with all my heart.

I feel an ache of confusion, but I'll deal with my treacherous feelings later. For now, the only thing that matters is him making it through another night.

"Please," I whisper, sending up a silent prayer. "Please let him live."

The next forty-eight hours pass in a blur of anxiety. I'm so worried about Sebastian that I can hardly stand it. He drifts in and out of consciousness, fighting a fever one moment and chills the next. During one of his brief periods of consciousness, I manage to move him up to his bedroom, although he's so out of it that I'm not sure he even realizes what's going on.

But the bed is more comfortable for him, and I pull a chair up close to his bedside, where I sit as I try to take care of him. It mostly consists of feeding him soup and keeping him hydrated with tea and water. I found Tylenol in the bathroom cabinet, so I keep giving him doses every four hours to help with the fever and body aches.

All I can do aside from that is pray.

To what God, I'm not sure, I just know, he has to make it. He has to be OK. The alternative…

It's unthinkable.

I tell myself it's just self-preservation talking: I need Sebastian alive and healthy to make it out of here. I don't know the roads, or how to call for rescue, and I have zero idea how the generator even works. All it would take is one more blizzard for me to freeze to death alone.

He's my means of survival, that's all.

But deep down, I know, that's not even the half of it. It wasn't self-preservation that sent me racing across thin ice to try and rescue him, or has spent sleepless nights at his bedside, praying he makes it through this OK.

No, my need for Sebastian is something deeper. Stronger. A connection I can't bear to think could be severed.

So what does that say about me?

"Avery...?"

Sebastian's voice filters through my hazy dreams. I wake, disoriented. Daylight is filtering through the bedroom windows, but I have no idea what time it is. I must have passed out again, in the rocker by his bed.

I blink, yawning, as it all comes filtering back into my tired mind. "Sebastian?" I blurt, panicked. He's been sleeping more soundly, but if he's mumbling and delirious again—

"I'm right here."

Sebastian's voice comes, calm. He shifts, sitting up in bed on his own, and when I search his face for signs of sickness, I find his eyes are clear, watching me. More alert than he has been in days.

Relief sweeps through me. "You're awake!"

I move closer and press my hand to his forehead. It feels normal. "Your fever has broken," I tell him, beaming.

Sebastian manages a faint smile. "About bloody time," he says, with a cough.

I quickly pass him a cup of water, and he takes a few sips.

"How do you feel?" I ask, still anxious.

"Weak. Hungry." He shrugs, giving me a rueful smile. "Like I took a long swim in a very cold lake."

"Understatement of the year."

Emotion swells in my chest, but I try to hide it. I get up and give a brisk nod. "I'll go get you something to eat."

I hurry out, but the second I'm downstairs and out of

earshot, I sag against the wall, my legs giving way as the sobs of sheer relief take over.

He's going to be OK!

I gasp for air, shocked at the force of my reaction. I didn't realize quite how terrified I've been of losing him, until now, the danger has passed.

It feels like a miracle. A reprieve, from the dark possibility of life without him.

I pull myself together after a moment, brushing the tears from my cheeks and pushing myself away from the wall. I head to the kitchen, and busy myself heating some chicken broth. We've gone through all the canned soup, and I don't want to waste time making any from scratch right now. After being at his side around-the-clock for the past two days, I'm not ready to be away from him for long. A small part of me is worried that he'll somehow regress if I'm not there.

Maybe it's not rational, but I'm finding that things rarely are when it comes to my relationship with Sebastian.

When I return to the room, he's emerging from the bathroom, hair damp like he just got out of the shower. I put the tray down quickly and hurry toward him.

"What are you doing? I could have helped you."

He waves away my concern. "I can piss by myself. Thanks."

"Don't be posturing, asshole." I manage, relieved he's back to his old acerbic self. "You're still weak, you can barely stand. Here," I guide him back to the bed, but Sebastian shakes me off.

"I said I can handle it."

"Would you just let me help?" I snap, covering my relief. "You're a terrible patient."

"Well, you're not winning any nursing awards," he shoots back, slowly pulling a fresh sweater over his head.

"This is the thanks I get, for saving your damn life." I make a show of rolling my eyes as I straighten up his bed things. "I should have left you splashing around in that lake."

"So why didn't you?"

Sebastian's question is quiet, and when I look over, the humor is gone from his gaze.

"Why didn't you just leave me there?" he asks again, his eyes burning into mine with unreadable emotion. "If you hate me so much, why didn't you walk away and let fate take its course?"

"Because I'd like to make it out of these mountains without frostbite, and you're the only one who knows where the fuse box is," I reply lightly, avoiding his gaze.

He's quiet for a long moment, and I can't resist the urge to look at him again. He's looking at me like I'm a complicated puzzle he's trying to put together.

"I don't believe you," he says simply.

"That's your prerogative." I reply, still flippant. "Now, eat your soup, and take it easy. I'll be downstairs."

"Avery." His voice stops me before I can leave, commanding. "Talk to me. Tell me the truth."

*The truth...*

I give a hollow laugh, whirling back to face him. "You want the truth? Fine." I exclaim, throwing my hands up in defeat. "I couldn't let you die. I thought about it," I add fiercely. "Believe me, I wanted to let you drown. Just slip away and be gone for my life for good. Maybe then, I'd have some fucking peace. But I couldn't. I couldn't do it!" I yell, remembering my terror at seeing him slip beneath the water. "You and me, we're connected now, however twisted that might be. I can't live with you, and I can't live without you. Is that what you wanted to hear?" I demand, shoving at his chest in anger. "Are you happy now?"

"No!" Sebastian yells back. "None of this is what I wanted.

Fuck, Avery, do you think I would have come after you if I had any choice in it at all? This is just about killing me, to know you hate me, but to still be consumed by you. Who the fuck would choose to live this way?"

*Me.*

"I don't hate you." The words slip out in a whisper, before I can stop them. My cheeks flush, and I look away at the reluctant confession. "Not anymore. I wish that I did," I add helplessly, feeling that treacherous ache in my chest, all the confusion and longing and echoes of anger mingling in a toxic cocktail. "It would make it all so much easier, but... I don't."

It wasn't hate that's kept me up these last nights, praying for his survival. Tending to him, willing him to pull through. It hasn't been hate in my heart, bargaining with the clouded skies, making a hundred deals with the devil, just to see Sebastian wake again.

*It was love.*

I stop myself from saying it just in time. That's just the panic talking; all the stress I've been through over the past few days. But when I look up, Sebastian is watching me with a new intensity burning in his eyes.

"I don't hate you either," he says, with an aching smile on his lips. "God knows I should, the way you've tormented me, but... When I was going under, when I thought it was the end... All I could think was that I had to survive. For *you*."

Oh God.

I don't think twice. I close the distance between us, throw my arms around his neck, and kiss him with everything I have.

Sebastian almost stumbles back in surprise, but then his hands are cradling my face, and his mouth is on mine, tongues tangling in a sensual, heady dance; not harsh, or punishing, the way it's been between us here at the cabin, but something softer.

Tender.

*Oh.*

I melt into him, and we tumble back onto the bed, suddenly hungry, starved for each other's touch. His hands are everywhere, and I arch against him, needing to feel him against me. Inside me. *Everywhere.*

I fumble with the waistband of his pajama pants, and Sebastian groans, already bucking his hard cock into my hand through the cotton fabric. "Baby," he breathes heavily, and the rasp in his voice reminds me just how close he's come to death. He's still getting his strength back, and as much as I want him pounding hard into me, I know we'll have to wait for that.

But that doesn't mean I can't have any fun…

I pull back, and lean above him, with a flirty grin. "Now, what did I say about taking it easy?" I murmur, stroking over his cock.

Sebastian groans again, his head falling back onto the pillows. "Don't torture me, I don't think I can take it."

"Oh, there's no torture here. I'm your nurse, remember? It's my job to take very good care of you…" I lean down and kiss his mouth again, teasing, as my hand slips inside his pants and slowly caresses his cock. It leaps in my hand, hard and thick, and I feel a shudder of lust spiral through me.

God, I want him.

"Avery…" Sebastian rasps again, reaching for me. His hands slide over my body, gripping my hips as he pulls me to straddle his lap. We make short work of my sweatpants and underwear, and then I'm poised there above him, eyes locked on his.

I lower myself onto him, sinking down onto his cock.

"Fuck, baby…" Sebastian hisses as I take him all the way to the hilt, and I moan in response, swaying against him. "Goddamn… You're so tight."

I clench around him, and another groan falls from his lips. "Please..." he mutters, "You can't—"

"Can't what?" I ask archly, flexing my inner muscles again. "Do *this*."

He growls, and grabs a handful of my hair, tightening his grip until I give a breathless mewl. "What are you waiting for, Sparrow?" he demands, giving me a look of dark passion, dropping blazing kisses along my throat. "Feel that?" he demands, voice low in my ear as he thrusts up inside me, stretching me wider, making me gasp. "Every inch is yours. Take it. Take it all."

So I do.

My heart pounding, my blood thick with desire, I slowly rise up and sink down on his cock again, taking him so deep it makes me moan. It feels incredible, not just the thick stretch of him, but the intensity of his gaze. Our eyes stay locked on each other, a shimmering intimacy building right here between us, something wild and overwhelming rising up inside me, driving me on as I move, rocking my hips back and forth, taking my pleasure just like he ordered.

"That's it," Sebastian groans, gripping my hips tighter, moving me on his lap. "That's my sweet, filthy girl."

I moan, tossing my head back as I rock against him, chasing the friction, and the perfect angle of his cock, hitting just right inside me. "Sebastian!" I cry, as he moves his hands to my breasts, caressing through my T-shirt. My nipples ache under his expert hands, my whole body winding tighter. I grind faster, panting. "Don't stop. Oh God, don't stop!"

"Never," he vows fiercely, thrusting up inside me, slow but perfect, every last inch. He tilts my head back down to look at him, holding my gaze as our bodies writhe. "You were made for this, weren't you, baby?" he demands, fucking me deep. Making me moan. "Made to take my cock and drive me out of my goddamn mind. My avenging angel... My good little whore."

His dark eyes burn into me, past all my defenses, and god, it's too much, too good to take.

"Seb!" I scream as my climax sweeps through me in a torrent of ecstasy. I spasm in pleasure, and Sebastian rears up, embedding himself inside me, coming with a cry that's swallowed by our fevered kisses. I feel the orgasm sweep through the both of us, surging, joining us somehow in this madness.

There's nothing I can do but hold onto him, and lose myself in the rush.

## Chapter 6

## *Sebastian*

I've never been a forgiving man.
 Fool me once, shame on you. Fool me twice?
 I'll burn your life to the ground.
So, when I realized that night at our engagement party that Avery had been living a lie... That she'd betrayed everything I thought was true about our love, I swore that she was dead to me.

Or at least, she soon would be...

It's funny, how staring death in the face myself changed everything about that bitter vow. The plane crash, my accident in the ice... Every time I thought it was the end for me, all I could think about was her.

Her fierce spirit. Her sweet song. The chaos of passion only she can drive me to, and above all else, the blessed relief I always feel in her arms.

It all became clear. This woman belongs to me, the same way my heart belongs to her. And I'm not the only one who's come a full 180. The look of terror in Avery's eyes when I plunged through the ice... The way she diligently nursed me back to health, holding me every night, and muttering the prayers she thought I couldn't hear…

You can't fake that kind of concern.

No, she feels it, too. Something's changed between us now. Out here in the wilderness, all of our former lies and betrayal have been stripped away. There's no place to hide, no point in pretending anymore.

All that's left is this bond between us. Inexplicable, but impossible to break.

I look out at the snowy vista, on the porch drinking my morning coffee. Avery is still upstairs, sleeping peacefully in my bed, as I check the weather conditions and terrain again. It's been clear for days now, and some of the snowfall has even melted, leaving the main road clearer, spiraling north through the mountains, towards where I know that there's a town a few hours' walk away.

There's nothing stopping us from leaving now. Hell, there's been nothing stopping us for the past couple of days, but I haven't said a word. I've told myself it's because I'm still getting my strength back, but that's a lie. I feel just fine now, thanks to Avery's tender care.

The truth is, I don't want to leave.

Here, I can pretend that the outside world doesn't exist. That the world doesn't know the truth about me, and the awful accident that claimed my father's life. Avery made sure it was splashed across every front page in the world: Sebastian Wolfe's killer past. And I don't doubt, the media frenzy will have only grown with our disappearance, and the plane going missing.

But it's not my empire, or riches that matter to me right now. No, it's the people I left behind. When I remember the way they all looked at me… My mother's shock, Richard's triumph, Bianca's tearful disbelief…

I can't bear it. They think I'm a monster.

I know, deep down, they're right.

There's a world of scandal and betrayal waiting for me out there, but here at the cabin, I can forget my ruin. Nothing matters but me and Avery, and the hours we spend talking, the nights of wild pleasure, and all her frenzied cries. If I could stay here forever with her, I would do it in a heartbeat—but I know that this can't last. We're starting to run low on provisions, and now that there's a thaw in the weather, it may be our only chance to leave for weeks. And if there's another blizzard or accident, if Avery is the one who gets sick or hurt?

I can't risk it.

If we're going to leave, we need to do it now.

I finish up my coffee and go upstairs. Avery has rolled over onto her stomach in her sleep, her hair a wild mess on the pillows and the blankets pushed down, leaving her bare back completely exposed.

I pause there in the doorway. I've never been accused of being a romantic or sentimental man, but I find myself watching her sleep, a sense of fierce protection burning deep inside. I know she has real feelings for me, whether she wants to or not. I can tell by the way she took care of me, nursing me back to health at the detriment of her own.

She was tender. Loving.

She cares about me.

I'd rather die than let anyone hurt her. And if I'm walking around with a target on my back...

How can I put her life at risk?

"Avery," I say softly.

She opens her eyes, yawning. "Where did you go?" she asks, with a sleepy, warm smile that strikes a bolt clean through my chest. "It's cold here without you."

I go sit on the edge of the bed. "I needed some coffee and little time to think."

"Sounds serious." She sits up, frowning a little.

I take her hand. "We need to leave," I say quietly. "Today. The weather's cleared for now, but if we wait any longer... We could be trapped here for months."

"Would that be such a bad thing?" she says playfully, and I sigh.

"No." I give her a reluctant smile. "But you'd probably change your mind once the pantry is bare and we're down to the canned asparagus."

"Ew," Avery gives a little giggle. "Good point."

"The nearest town is a full day's walk away," I continue. "If we leave this morning, we'll have plenty of time. It won't be like the first hike," I add. "The snow has melted, it'll be a straight shot along the mountain road."

She nods, slipping her arms around me. "I understand," she says, sighing into my ear. "I just... wish we could stay."

"I know, sweetheart." I wish it, too.

She doesn't speak for a long moment. I know that she's doing the same thing I was as I sat on the porch: Coming to terms with what we need to do.

"How are we going to get out of here?" she finally asks. "Have you been hiding a snowmobile somewhere that I don't know about?"

I chuckle. "Not quite. Have you ever been skiing?"

An hour later, we're dressed warmly in waterproof clothing, setting out along the mountain road. It's a clear, bright day, and the valley is muffled and silent with the snow, nothing but the swish of our skis on the untouched snow.

"I'm not sure about this," Avery says, still moving cautiously with the skis strapped to her boots.

"Skiing really isn't that hard," I reassure her, keeping my pace slow beside her. "You'll pick it up quickly."

"No, not that." She shakes her head, shooting me a concerned look. "You just got over being sick. Are you sure you're up for this?"

"Of course," I say, dismissing her concern. "You know first-hand just how good my stamina is these days," I add, and she gives another giggle.

God, I could listen to her laugh forever. It's only now that I'm realizing how little I know of the real Avery Carmichael. She's been playing a role with me for so long that these flashes of her true self are a revelation, the teasing and lightness I've only ever glimpsed before.

"OK, old man," she teases with a grin, picking up the pace. "Try to keep up!"

We set off along the road, moving faster than we did on our hike up. I keep a close eye on Avery, and she's a little unsteady at first, but she's a fast learner, and it's not long before we've crested the ridge at the top of the incline. "All downhill from here," I reassure her.

"Gee, that's a comfort," she quips back.

"You're a natural," I say, watching her. "Are you sure you've never done this before?"

Avery gives a sharp laugh. "Skiing? No, I wasn't wintering in Aspen," she retorts, sarcastic. "The closest I got was sledding upstate."

I ski in silence beside her for a moment. "So, the story you told me, about your father…"

She glances over. "It was a lie," she admits. "Well, kind of. He is dead," she adds. "He passed years ago, in the line of duty."

"He was a cop?"

She shakes her head. "A Barretti man."

I put two and two together. The night that I first met her, over that high-stakes poker game with mob boss Nero Barretti. I thought at the time I was stealing her away from him. Taking my rival's prize before he could enjoy her.

Now I know, she was pulling the strings, all along.

"You're part of Barretti's crew," I say, and she nods.

"I've known him most of my life. I grew up in that world, and after my mom took off, well, I made myself useful. Running the legit organizations," she explains, cheeks flushed from the cold and exertion. "Being the clean name on the liquor license."

"That's how you knew Miles."

I regret saying his name immediately. Hell, I regret everything about that man. Not because I should have stopped him gambling his life away like that—it was his choice to make—but because losing him caused Avery such pain.

I brace myself for a bitter comment, but instead, Avery just nods. "Yes. We were friends."

"Just friends?" I can't stop myself asking.

"Just friends," she confirms quietly. She looks straight ahead, skiing in silence for a moment over the powdered snow, then she adds. "I was in love with him, but... You were right. He didn't love me back. Not enough, anyway. Not enough to count."

I'm torn between guilt, and relief. Guilt, that Avery lost someone so close to her, and relief, that Miles was a damn fool who didn't realize what was standing right in front of him.

How that man could have known Avery, even for a single day, and not worshipped the ground she walks on...

"I'm sorry."

She stops skiing, looking over at me with a curious look on her face. "You've never said that before," she says quietly. "Not about Miles."

"Well, I am." I take a heavy breath. I'm used to regret and guilt—those feelings have gnawed away inside of me ever since the night of the crash, making me numb to the sensation. But now, with Avery, I feel them burning like new again.

For her.

"He made his choices, but... I'm sorry they caused you pain. If I could go back in time now and stop him from placing those bets, I would," I add honestly. "I'd turn him away from the game, and maybe then... Well, maybe everything would have been different for you."

Her jaw tightens, and an unreadable emotion flits across her face. "It's too late for that now, isn't it?"

Avery pushes off again, skiing ahead.

My heart sinks. Of course, she can't forgive me for what happened to Miles. Even with the thaw between us, I know, that blame will never die.

And I can't expect it to.

"Stick to the road," I call to her, as she moves faster, clearly trying to put distance between us. The trees are thick here, but I know, the terrain can turn deadly. "Avery, slow down."

I push off, skiing hard to catch up with her. The slope gets steeper, increasing our pace, and suddenly, we shoot out of the tree line and find—

A sudden cliff up ahead, with a perilous drop.

"Avery!" I yell, but she's going too fast to slow down.

"Seb!" I hear the panic in her voice, but she's not experienced enough to know how to veer away or to stop herself from hurtling closer.

Fuck.

Crouching, I angle my body and speed after her—heading straight for the edge of the cliff. Panic grips me, forcing me on, and at the very last minute, I manage to grab her arm and yank her into a hairpin turn, tumbling into a snowdrift in a tangle of limbs and skis.

Avery sits up, gasping for air. Her eyes widen, taking in the drop.

"Are you OK?" I demand, brushing snow off us. She nods, taking my hand as I pull her to her feet again.

"I guess we're even now," she says faintly. "I save your life... You save mine."

I exhale in a rush, relieved. That was close.

Too damn close.

"Come on," I tell her, hiding my panic. "We're getting closer."

"Right. No more exciting detours." Avery pushes off, skiing after me back to the road, but my nerves are still shaken, haunted by the image of her plunging straight for the sheer drop.

How am I supposed to keep this girl safe?

Someone was willing to blow up a plane—and kill Avery— just to get to me. The people I love always get hurt around me. My father. Scarlett. Now her.

If something happens to her, I'll never forgive myself.

"Look!" she exclaims, breaking into my dark thoughts. "Over there!"

I follow her pointing and see a scatter of lights in the distance. Houses, dotted in the valley, and the glowing lights of town.

"We made it," she cheers, beaming at me. "We're safe now."

I nod and follow her down the slope.

I don't have the heart to tell her that she may never be safe with me.

# Chapter 7
## *Avery*

After skiing all day, we reach the village just before nightfall. The first couple of houses we try are empty, but just as I'm about to collapse with exhaustion, we find one lit up and occupied by a friendly Swiss couple in their fifties, who welcome us in, and buy Sebastian's smooth cover story about a snowy road trip and engine trouble. They send us to sleep in their cozy guestroom, and even drive us to the local train station the next morning, to catch the direct train to Zurich.

"Now, this is the way to travel," I sigh in relief, sitting in the first-class carriage watching the snowy landscape blur past—outside the nice, thick windows. "Inside, on solid ground… with hot chocolate."

Sebastian chuckles. "Is that a hint for me to hit the café car?"

I bat my eyelashes playfully. "If you're heading in that direction…"

"I'll see if I can rustle up a sandwich or two."

He gets up, and goes to hunt and gather, while I sit back to enjoy the view. I'm ready to relax and put the stress of the past week behind me for the rest of the ride, but then a businessman in the seat across the aisle opens his newspaper, and I freeze.

Sebastian is on the front page.

It's an old photo of him, suave at some fancy event in a suit and tie, but there's no mistaking that icy stare. 'Killer Revelations Rock Wolfe Capital,' the headline reads.

I should have guessed. His scandalous arrest and our plane disappearance are still huge news. Even though we've been cloistered away from it all at the cabin, the rest of the world has been breathlessly speculating over everything they just learned.

Everything I told them.

I feel a pang of regret. I thought it would be a victory, exposing his involvement in that car crash when he was younger, but I already know, it was no victory at all. At least, not for me. Sebastian's uncle has been the one to profit, taking back control of his company, and I'm sure the rest of Sebastian's enemies are celebrating too.

He's a wanted man—and everyone thinks he's dead.

The carriage door slides open, and I see Sebastian returning with cups and packages of food.

Shit.

I bolt up, quickly grabbing our bags and hustling to meet him before the businessman can glance up and recognize him. "Not here," I hiss, leading him back to a different carriage. I practically shove him in the seat by the window, trying to block anyone's view.

"What's going on?" Sebastian frowns.

"You're all over the papers," I tell him grimly. "Photos everywhere."

He exhales. "Right. Of course I am."

I study him. With week-old beard growth, and too-long hair, he looks a little different... But who am I kidding? "It would help if you weren't so handsome," I grumble.

He arches an eyebrow, amused. "You think I'm handsome?"

I roll my eyes. "It's not a good thing. Someone's going to recognize you, before we even step off the train."

Sebastian rummages in his backpack and pulls out a knit cap and sunglasses. "Better?" he asks, pulling them on.

"A little," I agree. "But what about Zurich? It's the finance capital of Europe. And in case you've forgotten, you're kind of a big deal."

"Were," he corrects me. "They think I'm dead, remember? And we're going to keep it that way."

I nod. The train is slowing now, approaching the station, and we gather our things, joining the crowd that exits the train, and moves through the big concourse.

We emerge outside, to the busy central streets full of people, cars, and buildings. I blink. After the snowy isolation of the cabin, it's a shock to my system to be back in the middle of things again. "Where to now?" I ask.

"We're not safe," Sebastian replies, one hand already protectively on my back. "Never mind the media, if whoever set that bomb finds out I'm still alive..."

He doesn't finish the sentence. He doesn't have to.

"So what do we do?" I ask, swallowing hard. "We don't have money, or a place to stay. And you can't exactly use your credit cards, what with being dead and all."

Sebastian nods slowly, and I can tell, he's trying to figure something out. A man like that can't have many people he trusts with his life.

So it's a good thing I do.

"Come on," I tell him, spotting a phone booth nearby. "I need to make a call."

We cross the plaza, and I figure out how to reverse the charges to Nero in New York. My nerves are racing as I dial. I can only imagine what he's been thinking since the plane disappeared.

It rings and rings. Just when I think he's not going to answer, I hear a click and his gruff voice comes over the line. "Yeah?"

"Nero, it's me. Avery."

There's a long pause. "Bullshit." His voice is suddenly like steel.

Damn. Of course he's not trusting at the best of times, but now? "It's me, I swear it is," I insist. "Look, I don't have time, but... I know how you got that scar on your knee, the one from falling flat on your damn face after you stole your father's whiskey when you were twelve."

I hear Nero's hiss of breath at the old memory. "Avery?" he says it again, disbelieving. "Holy shit, they said you were dead."

"I almost was," I reply, with a glance to where Sebastian is pacing near the booth. "I don't have time to explain, but... I need help. We have to lay low until we can figure out who tried to kill Sebastian. Can you wire some money, and book a hotel? We're in Zurich."

"We..." Nero echoes. "You're with Wolfe?"

"Yes."

He doesn't ask anything more, thank God. Just gives a brief promise not to blow our cover and hangs up. I knew he'd come through for me. He's had his fair share of near-death experiences himself.

I step outside the booth and fill in Sebastian. "Nero's organizing everything for us," I tell him.

His lips twist, wry. "I figured he must be in on this. Let me guess, he threw that game of cards?"

I nod, wondering if he's mad about my lies. But Sebastian

just gives me a look. "I don't like cheating. One of these days, I'm going to need a rematch."

I almost laugh out loud at that. "Sure," I reply. "You, me, and Nero Barretti can sit around a card table and catch up."

Sebastian smiles back at me, too. Then the phone rings behind me and I go to answer. Nero has arranged a wire to a Western Union nearby, and a hotel in the central business district. "I booked it in your name," he says. "I figure, Sebastian's the only one splashed over the press right now."

"Thanks." I reply.

"Just be careful," he warns me. "Whoever the hell is coming after Sebastian, they have deep pockets. Everyone's bought the plane crash story, they all think you're both dead."

"Then hopefully, that will work in our favor. Nobody will be looking for us," I say.

"Nobody would be looking for *you*," Nero corrects me. "Avery—"

"I've got to go," I cut him off, before he says what I know he's thinking. "Thank you, I'll be careful. Talk soon."

I hang up and rejoin Sebastian. We pick up the cash, then head to the hotel. "You should wait out here while I check in," I tell him, glancing to the luxurious looking building. "They're less likely to remember a woman traveling alone."

He nods, and I head inside, Nero's words echoing in my ears.

It's Sebastian Wolfe the world knows—and hates. He could get recognized at any minute, and the people who tried to kill him with that explosion might come back to finish the job.

But me? I could slip away into the shadows and leave no trace behind. The Avery Carmichael I've been pretending to be these past months is just that: a fake. With a few keystrokes from Nero's hacker contact, Charlie, I could disappear again, and nobody would ever know I survived.

But I wouldn't be with Sebastian.

"*Guten tag*," the doorman greets me, and I try to pull myself together as I step inside the lobby. It's all gilt-edged and understated, just screaming money, so I try to look like I belong as I stride to the front desk and flash a smile.

"Room for Carmichael," I say, "I believe my assistant made the reservation."

The clerk searches the system. "Ah yes, we have you in the Rose suite. Will you be staying with us alone?"

"Yes," I lie, and show him my passport, which I kept since the crash.

"Very good," he nods, dealing with the paperwork. "You're on the third floor. Do enjoy your stay."

I take the keycard and walk slowly to the elevator. The doors are just about to close, when a hand stops them. "Apologies."

Sebastian steps inside, sunglasses still on, and his knit cap pulled low. "What floor?" he asks, as if we're strangers.

"Third," I reply, keeping my breathing even.

He hits the button, and we ride up in silence, as if we don't even know each other. We keep up the act as we step off the elevator, passing other guests in the hall. It's not until we're safely inside the room with the door locked and chained behind us that I exhale and pull him closer for a big hug.

"I kept waiting for someone to yell and stop us," I admit, holding him closer.

Sebastian strokes my hair. "We're safe, for now."

"But what about tomorrow, and the day after that?" I ask, my worries crashing back again. "Where can we go? What are we going to do?"

"We'll figure it out," Sebastian reassures me. "I have resources, the kind of money that can make anyone disappear."

"But how can we get to it?" I ask, still concerned. "You can't exactly stroll into a bank now or charge your credit cards. You're supposed to be dead!"

Sebastian nods, and I can see, he's thinking fast. "Right... Which means everything will be going to the beneficiary of my estate. All my money, property, everything passes to them on my death. They don't even have to wait for the probate to clear, half my assets are in special trusts, designed to get around all that red tape."

"And who's that?" I ask, hopeful.

"My sister, Scarlett." He looks grim. "She could walk into any bank in Zurich and stroll out with a suitcase of cash and gold, but... I don't want to ask her for help." He sighs, dragging a hand through his hair in frustration. "After everything she's been through... I can't pull her into this. It's not fair for her."

"Of course not," I agree immediately. We're both silent a moment, thinking again. Sebastian paces restlessly, like a trapped animal.

Then I get an idea.

"If we can't get Scarlett to walk in the bank and get your money... How about someone who looks like her?"

Our plan comes together in no time at all: I'll impersonate Sebastian's sister, present myself at the bank, and get us the cash we need.

"It might work," Sebastian says thoughtfully. "Nobody here will ever have met her, and the account is numbered: You only need a passcode to access it, not any kind of ID."

"Secret funds in a Swiss bank account," I tease, trying to keep things light. "You haven't been up to anything shady, I hope, Mr. Wolfe?"

He gives me a grin. "It's all perfectly legal. At least, according to my lawyers."

So, there's nothing stopping us now. I dye my hair to match Scarlett's dark brown color as closely as possible and go shopping for chic designer clothing with the money Nero wired, the more expensive the better. Zurich is packed with expensive stores, all dripping with luxury and elegance, but even in my snooty costume with massive sunglasses and a big leather purse, I'm still nervous. Sure, I've pulled off some impressive acting in the past, most notably when I convinced Sebastian that I was some meek and innocent woman that he could trust, but the stakes feel higher this time. Sebastian is wanted for murder.

Someone tried to kill us.

There's a lot of pressure to stay hidden.

"Are you sure I can really do this?" I ask anxiously, adjusting my disguise in the mirror of our hotel suite. "I don't look anything like her, you know. Not close-up."

"You only need to fool the bank staff," Sebastian says. His voice is reassuring, but I can see the worry in his eyes, too. "Scarlett hasn't been seen in public for years, you can pull it off."

Neither of us say what we're both probably thinking right now: I *have* to pull it off. Otherwise, there's no way for us to start over. No money to fund our escape.

We don't have a choice.

I gulp. "I wish you could come with me," I whisper, gripping his shirt.

He looks frustrated. "I wish I could, too. But this will be a walk in the park, I promise," he adds, as if seeing my nerves. "Just stride in there like you own the place, like this is no big deal at all."

"Sure," I mutter, adjusting my dress and blazer. "Because I go rob banks every other weekend."

Sebastian smiles. "Ask for the premier account liaison," he

adds, handing me the paper with all the passcodes written down. "It's his job to transfer whatever you want."

I tuck the paper in my massive leather bag and take a deep breath. It's showtime.

"See you on the other side."

My nerves grow during the cab ride to the bank, and by the time we pull up outside the tall, imposing building, they're tangled in my throat.

I get out, gazing up at the steel and glass, modern and chic —with stone-faced guards posted discreetly at the exits.

*You can do this*, I remind myself, as I approach the main doors. Hell, I fooled Sebastian about my true motives for long enough. I can charm a snooty bank clerk out of a few million, no problem.

Walking inside, I keep my head held high and my steps sure, just the way I would imagine a woman that grew up rich would carry herself. It doesn't really matter that Scarlett herself is a down-to-earth kind of woman who would never be seen dead in Chanel. All that matters is that these people believe I'm Sebastian Wolfe's sister and heiress.

Bored. Entitled.

*Rich.*

Inside, the place looks nothing like a bank. The lobby area is all gleaming marble and Eames chairs, like a luxury office building. A sleek receptionist comes to greet me, looking like a supermodel. "*Velkommen*," she says crisply.

"Uh, hi, hello." I say, trying to sound English. "Scarlett Wolfe. I need to talk to the premier account liaison?"

"Miss Wolfe..." Her eyes sweep over me, and in an instant, she transforms with a smile. "But of course, please, wait one moment."

She gestures me to one of the seats, where I wait anxiously, until the elevator doors slide open, and a slim blonde man wearing a double-breasted suit emerges. He's impeccably tailored, with a neat blond goatee, and a greasy smile. "Miss Wolfe, so lovely to meet you at last," he says, taking my hand to shake. "My name is Gunterson, I've been handling your brother's accounts. My condolences, of course. What a tragedy."

"Mmm," I murmur, not meeting his eyes. "Thank you."

"Please come with me."

Gunterson leads me to the elevator, and then up to the fifth floor, which is richly carpeted and full of polished wood accents, like something out of a stuffy member's club. He settles me in a luxurious, plush office that could double as an antique collection, and like magic, another slim, blonde model of an assistant brings in a tray of coffee and snacks on bone china, with fine silver cutlery.

"Now tell me, Miss Wolfe, how may I be of assistance? Excuse my lack of preparation," he adds, "There was no appointment on my books."

I give what I hope is a bored, careless shrug. "The trip was last minute, you know, skiing, shopping..." I examine my nails. "I thought that since I was here, I would do a little banking. I need some funds transferred from my brother's trust accounts."

"Of course," Gunterson agrees. "You have the necessary information?"

"Yes." I rummage in my bag, then present him with the paper. Gunterson scans it, then pauses.

"I don't believe we've done business with these accounts before. How much do you wish to transfer?"

"All of it."

He blinks.

*Fuck.*

"Indeed? That would be quite a significant withdrawal."

I feel his eyes on me, but I try not to wilt. "They're my own personal accounts," I lie. "All this mess around Seb's estate... I don't want to have to jump through hoops every time I want to take a little trip to Cartier. I figured it would be easier just to move the whole lot over." I shrug again. "I mean, it doesn't matter where it is, does it? The money belongs to me now."

"Indeed it does, Miss Wolfe." Gunterson folds the paper and gets to his feet. "If you'll excuse me, I shall make the arrangements."

"Great. Oh, and can I get some herbal tea in here?" I add, in an arch voice. "I'm on a detox. Caffeine is poison, you know."

"Right away."

He exits, and I gasp for air. *Christ.*

Does he know I'm lying to him?

My heart races in my chest, wondering with every passing minute if my cover is blown. What if he's off calling security right now, or worse still, the police? Am I about to be marched out in handcuffs and thrown in jail, for fraud, attempted robbery, impersonation—

"Miss Wolfe?" Gunterson returns. I gulp.

"Yes?" I force a smile.

"The transaction is complete." He hands me a printed document, but I barely glance at it, the words are all a blur in my secret panic. "Your funds have been transferred."

Oh my God.

I try not to let my relief show. "Fine," I say airily, as if transferring tens of millions is just another Tuesday to me. I rise to my feet and give a little yawn. "Thanks for your help."

"Of course," he nods obediently. "And may I say again, what a tragedy it was to lose Mr. Wolfe. Your brother was a great man."

A great man—and a great thief.

Because as I walk out of the building, trying my best not to break into a run, it sinks in what we just did.

We've just stolen a good chunk of Sebastian's fortune—and there's no way for them to ever get it back.

## Chapter 8

### *Avery*

When Sebastian laid out his plan for me, detailing the circuitous route I was to take after leaving the bank, I thought he was being paranoid. But as I hurry down the street and hail a cab, my heart pounding out of my chest, I follow his instructions to the letter. I have the taxi drop me in the shopping district, then weave through stores for another half-hour, making sure I'm not being followed.

Everything seemed fine at the bank, but how do we know they really bought it? What if this is some elaborate ploy, to get me to lead them right to Sebastian?

I try to keep my fears at bay. Nobody knows we made it out of that crash alive, I remind myself. Hell, the probably haven't even found the plane yet, we were so far off course.

We're ghosts. Invisible.

And now, finally, we can disappear for good.

When I'm finally sure I'm not being tailed, I catch a cab to the small restaurant where Seb and I planned to meet. It's a cozy little family joint, with dim lighting and private booths.

It's still early, so there aren't many people around, and I find Sebastian in the back, hidden from view in an intimate booth.

I slide in across from him, and grab the glass of wine he has waiting, practically gulping the whole thing down before I blurt, "It's done. They transferred the funds."

Sebastian exhales, and a smile breaks across his handsome features. "You did it," he says, squeezing my hand. "God, I could kiss you right now."

"So why don't you?" I smile back, victorious.

He leans over and captures my lips in a slow, sizzling kiss. "I could do a whole lot more than kiss..." he murmurs, finally pulling away.

I smile, looking around. "I mean, it's private here, but let's not draw any more attention than we have to."

Sebastian chuckles and settles back in the booth. "It all went smoothly?" he checks. "No suspicious questions?"

I shake my head. "The guy practically fell over himself to do what I asked. That's some A-plus service. Delicious cookies, too."

Sebastian looks relieved. "I was going out of my mind, worrying," he admits, and I smile, touched.

"Me too. Every time someone glanced at me, I thought for sure my cover was blown."

I tell him the whole story, from the moment I walked through the door, and show him the documents Gunterson gave me. We pause our celebrations long enough to order food, and champagne, and toast to a mission accomplished.

I swallow down the delicious bubbles, and take a deep breath, collecting myself. "So... You have the money now," I start, cautious. "What happens next?"

Sebastian pauses. "I have to disappear," he replies, heavier now. "I've thought it through, every possible outcome, but... I don't see any other way. Now that my past has been exposed,

I'm facing arrest and jail time if I ever show my face again, not to mention the mess of blame over the company… The crash…" he sighs. "Everyone thinks I'm dead. The smartest thing to do now would be to let them keep believing it."

"Start over," I say quietly.

He nods. "Thanks to your field trip this morning, I have every resource at my disposal again. I can get a new name, new documents, go anywhere in the world I choose."

He pauses and meets my eyes. Glittering. Full of promise.

"And you could come with me."

I inhale in a rush. I've been wondering about it, if his vision of the future included me in it, and here it is.

The offer of a lifetime.

My thoughts race, and I buy time, slowly eating some of my schnitzel.

"If we disappeared together, where would you want to go?" I ask finally.

"What do you want to see?" he shoots back immediately. "Mountains? Beaches? I know a little island in the Caribbean we could go."

I sigh, thinking of tropical beaches and shady palms. "That sounds like heaven."

"I could buy a yacht," he adds, smiling. "And we could sail around the islands, drinking fresh coconut juice, and making love all day."

I laugh. "Are we planning a getaway or a porn movie?" I tease.

"Why not both?" Sebastian laughs. "But I mean it. We could go anywhere. Do anything. There's nothing stopping us. All you have to do is say the word."

"Disneyland?" I tease.

He smiles. "Just call me Mickey."

I laugh. We keep talking like that as we eat, spinning a one fantasy after another about where we could go. A resort in the mountains where we could see all the stars in the clear sky. A surf shack in Costa Rica, right on the shore.

"I mean it," he says, looking across the table at me. "As long as we're together, that's all that matters to me."

I pause, wanting to believe him. But even after everything that's happened, I can't be sure.

"You would trust me?" I ask softly. "After what I did to you?"

Sebastian holds my gaze. "Yes."

My disbelief must be clear, because he gives a regretful smile. "I'm not exactly innocent here, am I? We've both sinned against each other," he says. "We've both done some unforgiveable things but... It's different now. There's no lies between us anymore. We can put the past behind us now. We have a chance for a blank slate. If you want it."

And I do.

The already know the answer, I feel it pounding with every heartbeat. I belong with him. Wherever—and whoever that might be.

"Yes," I whisper. "I want it. A fresh start for us."

Sebastian kisses me again, but this time, there's no holding back, despite the people around to see us. He pulls me flush against him in the booth, his body taut against me and his tongue plunging deep between my lips like he's claiming me as his own. My blood ignites, and my body aches, and soon I'm gasping, panting for more.

"Seb..." I whisper hoarsely, pressing closer.

"Yes, Sparrow..." he answers, a teasing smile on his lips.

He has one hand draped around my shoulder, and his fingertips are caressing the back of my neck. Soft, so soft it makes me shiver with desire, my body coming alive for him.

*Only him.*

I wet my lips, cheeks already flushed and hot. The things he's already taught me... The ways this man has made me moan. I'm restless from the thought of it. His hands, his words, the way he can command and captivate me, like I belong to him.

His to control.

"I want another lesson."

My quiet confession makes his hand still, but just for a moment. Then he's pulling me to my feet, throwing a wad of banknotes on the table, and hustling me to the exit so fast, I almost stumble on my unsteady feet.

I'm not sure how we make it back to the hotel, but the moment the door closes behind us, he's on me, shoving me back against the wall and kissing me hard until the world is blotted out under the force of his passion and I'm writhing in his arms.

"Fuck, you need it, don't you baby?" Sebastian pins my wrists above my head, looking down at me with a dark possession in his gaze. I struggle uselessly against his iron grip, pressing my thighs together as his domination makes me ache.

"Yes," I gasp, arching towards him. "Please."

"Look at you, being so sweet for me..." Sebastian muses, trailing a hand over my body, teasing at my nipples and curling over my hip. "I remember when you swore you couldn't stand my touch."

"I was lying," I moan as his hand slips up the inside of my thigh, skimming closer to my aching core. "I always loved it. Even when I hated you, I wanted more."

"I know." Sebastian growls, low in my ear. He nips my lobe, making me gasp. "I know just how wet it made you, begging on your knees. The way this sweet cunt clenches for me..."

I moan again, desire blazing deep inside me as his fingers press me lightly through my panties. I go up on my tiptoes, eagerly pressing closer.

Needing more.

Sebastian chuckles. "Is *this* what you want?"

He presses, a little harder, rubbing my clit just right.

"*Yes,*" I whimper, lost in the wicked rhythm and the pleasure it sends spiraling through me. "Oh God, Sebastian, don't stop!"

"Hmm…" Sebastian's murmur is throaty in my ear. "I'm not so sure you're ready yet. You wanted a lesson, didn't you? Well, maybe what you need to learn is *patience*."

He moves his hand away, and I sob in protest. I'm close, so close…

"Shh, my sweet," he strokes hair from my eyes, watching me twist against his hold with satisfaction. "I want to look at you."

I draw in a ragged breath as Sebastian strips me, dragging my blazer off and pulling my dress over my head in a few swift movements. It's not long before I'm standing there in my panties and bra. Then he disposes of them, too, and I'm naked. Totally bared to his ravenous gaze.

"Beautiful," he growls appreciatively. "The sight of you… I really shouldn't be selfish, should I? A view like this deserves to be admired… by *everyone*."

Before I can even ask what he means, Sebastian takes my hand and leads me across the hotel room, to the wide swathe of windows looking out on the square below. We're not on a high floor, and we're close enough to the ground for me to be able to see the individual people going about their business below us: walking home from work, stopping at the bars nearby, out with the dog on an evening stroll.

"Hands against the glass," he orders me, pushing me into position right there, naked up against the glass. "Spread your legs for them, baby. That's right. Give everyone a look at that sweet pussy."

I gasp in shock—and excitement. *Is he really…?*

"I said, spread your fucking legs."

I shiver at the steel in his voice and do as he tells me. The glass is cool against my palms, and as I widen my stance on Sebastian's orders, he presses me even closer, so my bare breasts are pressed up against the glass.

Naked. Exposed. On display, for anyone to see.

*Oh God.*

The thrill and shame of it mingle in my blood, intoxicating, and I draw in a labored breath, already trembling in anticipation.

Behind me, Sebastian chuckles. "Look," he orders me, nodding to where a man has paused on the sidewalk outside the hotel. He's glancing up, directly at us. My core clenches. He can't really see me…

Can he?

"The glass is one way," I mumble, desperate for an explanation. "He can't see anything. Not really."

Sebastian laughs. "Do you really believe that?" he asks, his voice thick with satisfaction. "Or do you think he's enjoying the view?"

Fuck.

A rush of heat suffuses my bloodstream, and I shudder, close to coming before Sebastian even lays a hand on me.

How does he know how to turn me on like this?

How can he read my mind, and know all the filthy, forbidden desires that I'm hiding?

"Now that you have the spotlight, I think your audience deserves a show," Sebastian muses, reaching around to skim his hands lightly over my naked body. I sink back against him, sandwiched there between the glass, lost to the rush.

"What do you think, Sparrow?" Sebastian coos. "Should I put you on your knees, and make you suck my cock for them?

Show them how pretty you look with my dick in your mouth, choking down every inch?"

*Yes.*

I moan, arching into his touch.

"Or maybe they'd like to see this ass get nice and rosy," Sebastian continues, slipping a hand over my hip, and landing a sharp slap on one cheek. "I could take you on all fours, right here. Fuck you like an animal, mark you with my cum."

I whimper. I can't help it. God, the images he's conjuring.

The way I would submit to every whim.

"Or maybe, you want to be my whore tonight," he muses, his hand moving again, between my legs, to toy and tease with my swollen nub. "To bend over for me and take this cock any way I want; screaming the roof off for a good, hard fuck."

"Yes," I sob, writhing against his hand now, chasing the sweet friction. "Sebastian, *please.*"

He takes his hand away.

"You're feeling empty, baby?" he taunts me, still utterly in control. I can feel his thick erection pressing stiffly into my ass, but Sebastian just grinds it there, making me wait.

Making me beg.

"Please," I whimper again, dizzy now with longing. "I need you inside me. Filling me up."

"You mean, like this?"

Sebastian slips two fingers inside me, barely dipping into my wet pussy. I moan, thrusting back against them, trying to take him deeper, but he shoves me forward, face-first against the glass, trapping me in place. I sob in protest.

"I thought this was what you wanted," he taunts me, inching his fingers just a little deeper, but still, nowhere deep enough. "Me… Inside you… Filling you up…"

"*Sebastian!*" I cry, clenching around him in frustration. He chuckles.

"Shh, my sparrow. If you want more, you'll need to work for it. Get yourself off on my fingers, and then, maybe if you're a good girl, I'll reward you with my cock."

*Fuck.*

I clench again, desperate this time, thrusting my hips back to try and take more of his fingers. It's not enough, god, especially not compared to the thick invasion of his cock, but I work myself on them, panting, clenching, trying to chase that sweet release. "Please," I gasp, gyrating back, fucking myself on his teasing fingers as my breasts sway against the glass. "Oh god, please, *please*...."

"You beg so sweetly for me, baby," Sebastian growls. His breath behind me is labored now, and I can feel, he's losing some of his own iron control. "God, I could listen to you like this all night long."

"Sebastian!" I cry it again, louder. Fuck, I'm getting close now, but my climax is still just out of reach. "I need you. I need...."

"What do you need, my sparrow?" Sebastian thrusts his fingers deeper, slamming me up against the glass.

"Fuck me, please," I cry, long past sense or reason. All that matters is the craving deep inside, and the precipice of pleasure taunting me with every thin curl of his fingers against my walls. "I need you, rough and deep, like you said. Fuck me senseless!"

Sebastian stills at my desperate plea, and I feel his cock leap, pressed against my ass.

"Be careful what you wish for," he murmurs.

Then he releases me for a moment, and I hear the blissful sound of his belt snap, and the drag of his zipper as he shoves his pants down.

*Yes.*

I barely have time to catch my breath before he kicks my

legs wider, angles my hips, and thrusts into me from behind in one thick, ruthless stroke.

I cry out, my pleasure echoing in the dim hotel room as Sebastian grinds up, higher, fucking me all the way to the hilt.

"Tap three times on the glass if it's too much for you," he orders me, and then before I can even ask what he means, he brings one hand to rest, heavy around my throat.

*Oh my god.*

He thrusts into me again, hitting that perfect spot, and just the weight of his palm there, full of dark promise, sends me suddenly hurtling over the edge. I come with a cry, my body spasming in pleasure as my climax shatters through me.

But Sebastian is only just getting started.

"That's right, darling," he growls, picking up the pace of his thrusts, fucking me right through my orgasm and into the madness beyond. "You feel it, don't you, what's coming for you next."

The hand at my throat tightens. I moan, out of my mind with the illicit thrill. *The power...*

"Sebastian—"

"You're mine," he curses, breath ragged in my ear. His hips jerk in a punishing rhythm, his cock stretching me open, burying deep with every wild thrust. "Your pleasure belongs to me. Your obedience. *The very air you breathe.*"

He squeezes tighter, applying pressure on the sides of my neck. I'm lightheaded now, gasping, every nerve and sense in my body lit up and radiant as he takes his fill of me. I sink back, limp and mewling in his arms as he fucks me. Chokes me. Owns me, body and soul.

I couldn't fight it if I tried.

I'm his. Completely.

It's incredible. A surrender like nothing I've ever felt before. The lights of the city blur with the stars in my eyes, as

I'm overwhelmed with sensation, pleasure so thick and sweet in my veins, I could drown in it.

"I've got you, baby," Sebastian groans in my ear, as I sink into the glittering rush. "I've got you. Just let go."

His grip on my neck suddenly loosens, and there's a rush of blood so exhilarating, I shatter again.

"Seb!" My orgasm crashes through me, and I come with a fierce cry that seems to echo through the night, mingling with Sebastian's own curse of pleasure as he buries himself deep, and climaxes with a roar, leaving the both of us collapsed against the window, gasping at the lights below.

And I know that I never want to let go.

# Chapter 9

## *Avery*

When I wake the next morning, I'm alone in the bed.

"Sebastian?" I murmur, bleary-eyed. I lift my head and look around the room, wondering if he's gone to get us coffee or some breakfast.

I need it. The ache of last night is still echoing in my limbs, a bone-deep pleasure that makes me sigh in satisfaction. I yawn happily, hoping he comes back soon—with something baked and delicious.

Then I see the envelope propped on the nightstand.

I sit up, already feeling a chill spread through my body, replacing the sleepy haze. I take a slow breath, bracing myself, and reach to open it.

A stack of cash tumbles out, and an American passport. My photo, with a fake name.

And a note. Just a few short words, in Sebastian's unmistakable handwriting.

*'You're free now.'*

And I realize in horror that he's gone

## Chapter 10

### *Sebastian*

I keep to the shadows, loitering in the alleyway across from the hotel. I know I should be long gone by now, out of the country, leaving Sebastian Wolfe dead and gone, but I can't. Not yet.

Not until I see her safely leave.

The glass door swings open, and a doorman leaps to help a guest with her bags.

Avery.

*Fuck.* She's dressed simply, but I can see, she's been crying, even from behind those massive sunglasses on her face. I can only imagine her reaction when she found me gone, leaving only that note and the fake ID I called in all kinds of favors to have messengered to the hotel, late last night.

She says something to the doorman, and he hails her a cab. I wonder where she's heading now.

I hope it's far. Back to New York, or even further still. Using the money I gifted as a fresh start, someplace she can forget she ever met me.

Somewhere I know, she'll finally be safe.

A cab draws up, and the doorman loads her bags. Avery pauses on the curb for a moment, glancing up, across the street towards me, like she can sense me here, watching.

I freeze, even though I know she can't see me, feeling her searching gaze like a bolt through my chest. I have to fight the gravity that pulls me to her. Wishing I could close the distance between us.

Wishing it didn't have to be this way.

But it does.

I stay hidden in the shadows as she finally turns away and gets into the cab. I hear the doorman instruct the driver to take her to the airport, and then the car pulls away.

I exhale. It's for the best, I vow, turning away. Being close to me has brought her nothing but pain since the day we met, and now I know somebody is out to kill me...

I can't take the risk of them hurting her, too. The plane crash was too close. What if next time, we're not so lucky?

I may have done some terrible things in my time, and learned to live with the guilt and shame, but I already know, I couldn't bear it if anything happened to Avery.

I have to leave her, there's no other way.

Even if it breaks my fucking heart.

# Chapter 11

## *Avery*

I head to the airport, and board my flight in a daze, too distant to even care if the airline staff look twice at the fake passport I'm traveling under.

But they don't.

I sail through first class check-in and security, and it's not long before I'm settled in the plush cabin, twenty-thousand feet above the earth, leaving Europe behind.

"Ma'am, may I bring you anything?" the attendant asks me.

I shake my head, my red eyes still hidden behind sunglasses. "No, thank you."

The man retreats politely, leaving me alone with my thoughts—and the piercing ache lodged deep within my chest.

*He left me.*

Maybe I shouldn't have been so surprised to wake up alone in that hotel room, with only memories of the closeness and wild passion we'd shared. After all, my relationship with Sebastian has been marked by lies upon lies, secret agendas, and hidden motives from the very beginning. But the past week we've spent together after the crash, I thought it was different now. That we were being honest, and open. Risking our hearts for real this time.

I was wrong.

I swallow back the ache, too sharp to stand. I look around and wave the flight attendant back. "Sorry," I blurt, "But I'd love a drink. Whiskey. Neat."

"Of course, Miss Michaels."

I blink, and it takes me a moment to realize, that's the name on my ticket, and that fake ID that Sebastian arranged.

I pull the passport from my purse, and glance at the pages. *Amelie Michaels.*

It's close to my old name, but someone else entirely. But of course, it has to be. Everyone thinks that Avery Carmichael is dead, buried in the snow somewhere in the Alps, the victim of a terrible plane crash.

A crash that was no accident...

I shiver, tucking the passport away as the steward delivers me my drink. "Thank you."

I take a gulp, feeling the low, sweet burn of the alcohol slipping down my throat.

So, this is what it feels like to be a ghost...

I feel an unfamiliar surge of grief. It shouldn't be so weird for me; I'm not leaving anything real behind. I've been living a lie for months now, and the Avery who was living in London with Sebastian was a fictional creation: fake background, fake personality, fake everything. I created her to achieve a goal, nothing more. It should be easy to leave her there, buried in the snow.

It should be a relief. A sordid chapter of my life is over. I kept my promise to Miles' memory. I got my revenge on the great Sebastian Wolfe.

But at what cost?

The grief cuts at me, and I drain my whiskey glass, trying to numb the pain. But I know, there's no drink in the world that could soothe my heartache.

*Why did he leave me?*

I know that he probably thinks he's being noble. Protecting me and keeping me safe and far away from whatever forces are trying to cause him harm. He's got a target on his back, after everything he's done, and it's not so easy for him to disappear. If anyone recognizes him out there....

It's game over.

Or maybe I'm just being the fool I always swore I never would be. Maybe those teasing plans we made were nothing but fantasy, and Sebastian always planned to walk away.

It was only fate that stranded us together at the cabin, after all. Only necessity that brought us together against the elements. He'd vowed to destroy me after I ruined his life; maybe that anger was too strong to be overcome, and once we were back in civilization again, and he had the chance to leave...

He took it, without a second thought. Absolving his conscience with those million bucks, like I was some high-priced whore he could fuck and pay off the next morning.

Maybe he's celebrating my broken heart.

"Ladies and gentlemen, we'll soon be approaching JFK..."

I startle back to reality, wiping tears from my eyes I didn't realize I was crying.

Whatever his reasons, it's over now. Our time together, my quest for vengeance, it's all behind me, and I have to try and think clearly now and be grateful for the way things turned out.

I'm home. Sebastian is in my past now. And I'm lucky to have gotten out of this alive.

But there's one question that haunts me, as the New York City skyline comes into view.

*What do I do now?*

. . .

I clear customs at JFK, and take a cab into the city, straight to Nero's club downtown. It's always been a regular Barretti haunt, a place for our crew to unwinds and do business, but I'm surprised to find, I don't recognize a single person in the place when I walk in. It's all trendy hipsters and craft cocktails, and when I make my way to the bar, the guy there just gives me a blank look.

"What'll it be?" he asks, sporting a pinstripe vest and an old-time moustache that Nero would have cut straight from his face with a penknife, if he ever saw it.

"I'm looking for Nero," I reply, glancing around.

The guy frowns. "Nero who?'

Is he kidding me?

"She means Barretti," the other bartender leans over. "Sorry, kid's new."

"Everything looks new," I remark, looking around the room. "Do you know where I can find him?"

The man shrugs. "Sorry, he doesn't come around here often. Maybe try his offices?"

*Right.* I realize too late that Nero must have moved his business operations to his fancy new construction project downtown. No more back room mafia deals. The man's gone legit.

"Thanks," I mutter, and head out, past a group of coeds cooing about how 'gritty' and 'authentic' the 'vibes' are here.

I wince. If they only knew what had gone on in these back rooms...

And those aren't the only changes. As I stroll the ten blocks to Nero's new digs, I can't help feeling like I've been away from the city for ten years, not just a few months. Everything feels different—or maybe I do. The brisk pace of pedestrians on the sidewalks, the noise and hustle of traffic in the streets...

*You've been acting like a pampered princess too long,* I scold myself, walking faster. This is what months in Sebastian's luxurious world has done for my street smarts: made me softer. Weak.

Well, there'll be no more of his lavish gifts now.

*No more nights crying out in pleasure, begging for Sebastian's domination and release...*

I find Nero's building shiny and buzzing with activity, like any other corporate tower in New York. His offices are on the top floor, with sweeping views of the city, and I find him still in some kind of meeting, gathered around a conference table with smart looking people in suits poring over spreadsheets.

He paces, commanding the room, just as much a leader as I've always known him, but this time, outfitted in a designer suit.

The mafia boss turned businessman.

Nero turns and sees me through the glass, and lights up. He gestures for me to join him, dismissing everyone else with just a few words.

"Avery!" he strides over, pulling me into a hug. "Shit, look at you! When did you get back?"

"Just now," I reply. "And technically, it's Amelie," I tell him. "Avery Carmichael is still missing, presumed dead."

"I know what that's like," Nero says with a knowing grin. "You OK?" He steps back and takes a long look at me, as if he's trying to assess for injuries.

"Yes. No. I don't know," I admit with a sigh. Seeing my old friend like this is opening the floodgates, and I don't know how much longer my resolve will hold.

Nero sees it and gives my shoulder a squeeze. "Let's go. I know Lily will want to see you. We'll order in, make a night of it. You can bring us up to speed on your adventures," he adds, and I give a hollow laugh.

"How much time do you have?"

"How about three extra-large pepperonis from Gino's?" Nero shoots back. "Will that be enough time?"

"Not even close."

We pick up those pizzas, and head back to his place, where Lily is just as happy and relieved to see me. We settle in with drinks and the food, and I fill them in on my time in Europe over the last few months. No holds barred.

When I'm done, Lily takes my hand and squeezes it sympathetically. "Oh, Avery…"

"It's stupid, I know," I say, trying not to crumble. I stare down at the greasy slice in my hand. "I mean, what kind of future could we have really had together? After all the anger, and lies, and revenge… That's not exactly the foundation for a beautiful love affair, is it?"

"Oh, I don't know…" Lily shoots Nero a glance, and they share a private smile. Then Nero gets serious again.

"I'm just glad you made it out of there alive. You've been meddling in dangerous shit," he warns me. "The fact someone was willing to blow your plane out of the sky, just to get back at Sebastian… You were right about the guy from the start. He's dangerous."

I swallow back a protest, I don't know why I feel the urge to defend him, but I do.

Lily shoots me a look. "Didn't you have some business you needed to finish up?" she asks Nero sweetly.

He frowns.

"Important business," Lily continues meaningfully. "In another room, while us girls talk."

"Right." Nero gets up—and grabs the last of the pizza.

"Hey!" Lily protests, but he just grins.

"That important business is hungry work," he teases, before exiting the room, and leaving us alone.

I feel a pang, just seeing their closeness and affection. Did I really think that I could have that same intimacy with Sebastian?

Did I really think it would last?

"So..." Lily pours us more wine and gives me a supportive smile. "You really think it's over?"

I nod.

"I can't believe I fell in love with the man," I tell her sadly, sinking back into the couch cushions. "I tried not to. I mean, I *hated* him."

"You know what they say," Lily says softly. "There's a fine line between love and hate."

"I guess you'd know a thing or two about that, huh?" I comment.

She smirks. "I could write a book about it. That's the thing about strong emotions... They get complicated. Passion and fury... Lust and loathing... Maybe they trigger the same instincts inside us. I don't know."

I sigh mournfully. "It would be easier if I could go back to hating him, but... I know him too well now. I know how much more there is to him than just the villain."

How much more there is of him to love.

"I just wish I could talk to him," I add, hopelessly. "Figure out how we could get through this, together. I know I could convince him, make him see..."

"But that's not what he chose, is it?" Lily points out gently. "I hate to say it, but it takes the both of you to be together. He left, without letting you know where he was going, or even what name he's using now. That's pretty clear, as far as breakups go."

"He ghosted me," I realize, with a sharp laugh, "The man literally ghosted me!"

Lily squeezes my shoulder again. "Maybe it's for the best," she offers. "He's wanted for murder, his empire is in ruins... He won't be coming back. Maybe he knew that it's time for the both of you to move on."

My heart aches. It sounds so simple, to put the past behind me, but what if I can't?

What if all I want is him?

## Chapter 12

### *Avery*

"*Take it, baby. Take every inch.*" I moan. Seb is behind me, his hand fisted in my hair as he drives his cock into me. I'm on my hands and knees, groaning in pleasure with every sharp thrust. "That's my good girl. Fuck, you take it so well…"

"Yes… Yes!" I'm so close to my orgasm, and he can tell. He keeps slowing down just as I'm about to come, drawing it out. It's a delicious torture that's driving me crazy.

"Seb… Please…" I beg.

"What is it, Sparrow? What do you want?"

I open my mouth to respond, to tell him that I want him to take me harder, to show me that I belong to him. I want him to touch and taste every part of me. I want to come so badly…

BEEP. BEEP.

An insistent noise breaks through my haze. "Sebastian…" I moan, still half-conscious. "Don't stop. Don't ever stop…"

BEEP.

Dammit. I wake breathless and drenched, still on the edge of release.

But Sebastian's not here. I'm alone in a dark bed.

It was all just a dream.

Cursing under my breath, I grasp around for the phone on my nightstand. It's a new one, I only just got it, and I can't imagine who has the number.

"Are you interested in a low-interest home loan?"

*Fuck.*

I hang up, collapsing back onto the pillows as my heart rate slowly returns to normal. But still, my body aches for Sebastian.

His steely touch, his groaned orders, his wicked tongue....

My hands slide lower, as if of their own accord. Down under the waistband of my pajama pants, to where I'm wet and needy for him.

*"That's my good girl..."*

I try to lose myself in memories again. Flashes of our nights together: at the sex club... in his London house... at the cabin...

But nothing can get me there, not without him.

Dammit.

Eventually, I give up, and go take a shower and prepare for the day ahead. I'm back in my old apartment on the Lower East Side, modest and sparsely decorated with old mementos and busted furniture. I never cared all that much about my surroundings or put effort into décor and clothing like some people, but now, my old place doesn't feel like home to me.

None of this does.

I stand in front of the mirror and wipe the condensation away with my hand. I barely recognize the woman standing there, and that's not just because my hair still dyed Scarlett's color.

Who am I anymore?

Miles' death changed me—and then my mission for revenge took me even further from the life I knew. I'm not even operating under my own name anymore, I realize, when I dress and grab my wallet, finding that passport still in my purse: my only identification now. And the printed document, showing the transfer to an account in my name. A million dollars I still can't believe is real.

Is this the new beginning Sebastian promised me?

Alone in a city far from him, with no idea what to do with myself?

*Get it together,* I instruct myself, yanking my hair back, and pulling a pair of my old boots from the closet. I've never been someone to sit around, moping, not when I can take action instead, so I head out, going to meet Nero for breakfast at one of our usual haunts near the club.

"I bet you missed these in England," he jokes, lifting one of the famous bacon, egg, and cheese sandwiches at the hole-in-the-wall diner we always like to go.

I manage a smile. "I don't know…" I tease back. "Sebastian's private chef made a mean blueberry pancake."

Nero snorts. "Now I see, you've gotten soft in the lap of luxury. Trading caviar for corn-dogs won't be so easy now, huh?"

I pause.

"Hey, I was only kidding," Nero adds, seeing my conflict. "I know, it'd take more than a few fancy dinners to change the Avery I always knew."

"Really?" I sigh. "Because I'm not exactly feeling like myself these days," I admit, taking a long sip of coffee.

Nero nods, slowly chewing his breakfast. "Makes sense," he says at last. "You spent a long time over there, it's only natural you grew connected. Happens to spies, too," he adds, "Undercover cops… Anyone maintaining a fictional life, the lines start to get blurred."

"So how do I get back to how it used to be?" I ask.

He gives a rueful shrug. "Time, I guess. What's next for you?"

"I don't know. That's part of the problem," I explain. "After Miles... Well, you know what happened. I was so consumed by my vengeance for so long, that I haven't even thought about what comes now."

I look down at my food, avoiding Nero's scrutiny. If I'm honest, I didn't think about what happened when I got back, because a small part of me wasn't sure I would ever make it out of my mission alive.

I was willing to die to have my revenge on Sebastian.

I just wasn't expecting life to go on, like nothing had happened.

But Nero understands life-and-death stakes better than anyone. "You want to know how I felt, the day after we sealed the deal with the Kovacks?" he asks suddenly, referring to the rival gang the Barrettis were at war with—and recently negotiated a ceasefire that bought him out of the game forever.

"How?"

"Lost," Nero replies, with a small grin. "Fuck, I didn't know what to do with myself. My whole life, I'd been a Barretti. Preparing to take the reins, then running shit... This was my life. My world."

"Until Lily," I say quietly, and he nods.

"She was a big part of it, but I set things in motion long before she came back into my life. Turning the Barrettis legit with the real estate deals, getting our guys off the streets," Nero says. "Because I knew, I couldn't go on like this. So, yeah, change is scary," he says, giving me a twisted smile. "It's fucking terrifying to have to switch things up, when you only ever know one life. But it's necessary. Sometimes, you just have to bite the bullet."

"Hopefully, not literally," I quip, and he laughs.

"Yeah, that's one of the advantages to the real estate game. The meetings are boring as hell, but I don't need to ride around with a piece in the glove box."

Nero reaches across and steals the rest of my food.

I take a deep breath. "You're right."

"I know."

I glare and slap his hand away from my home fries. "I mean, about starting over. I need to move on with my life now, whatever that means. Since apparently, my job at the bar has been filled," I add, giving him a look.

Nero winces. "Yeah, sorry about that. But if you want anything else, let me know. I can find you whatever you want at the company. Marketing, management, bossing around the boys on the construction site... Just say the word."

"Thanks," I say slowly. I didn't tell him and Lily about the money Sebastian left for me. I haven't decided if I want to touch it yet.

Or if it's too tainted: his payoff, so he could walk away guilt-free.

"I'll let you know," I tell him.

Nero checks his phone, then throws some money down. "I have to get to the site, but swing by the office later, yeah? I'll introduce you to the team. But don't beat yourself up for not having it all figured out just yet," he adds, resting a hand on my shoulder. "You've been through a lot this year. These things take time."

I nod and watch him leave. Nero Barretti, no longer the most feared mob boss in town. He seems to have hit the ground running in his new life, and I can tell that there's a weight lifted from his shoulders. He's happier now. Free from the crime and death that haunted our lives. It's clear, he wants that same new beginning for me, too.

But he has Lily beside him. And I'm all alone.

. . .

I linger a while longer over my coffee, turning ideas over in my mind. Do I want to go back to school, the way I pretended to for Sebastian? Pursue my music for the first time, or even just travel, and see the world?

With Sebastian's money, I could do anything.

Anything except bring him back to me.

Eventually, I get up to leave, but I'm just exiting the diner when I see someone I recognize, passing on the street.

"Wait... Charlie?" I call, in disbelief.

She turns, and I gape. She looks totally different to when I met her in London. Instead of the leather jacket and dark eyeliner of the expert hacker, she's dressed like a chic socialite, all Chanel and pearls, with a preppy little headband holding back sleek, dyed-red hair.

"Avery." She moves closer, and air-kisses me on both cheeks. "Darling, so good to see you."

My jaw drops even wider, then she laughs. "God, your face right now! Don't worry," she says, dropping the arch, breezy tone. "I'm on a job right now. Blending in. What do you think?" she says, doing a spin. "Butter wouldn't melt, huh?"

"It's creepy," I say, impressed.

"I was actually coming to find you at the bar," Charlie continues. "Nero said you were back in town, and I wanted to see if you'd followed up on my tip."

"Tip?" I echo, confused.

"I emailed you, a couple of weeks ago."

I give a laugh. "I've been kind of busy, in case you didn't keep up with the news."

"Right, dying in a fiery plane crash and all." Charlie looks amused. "Anyway, you should know, I found your forensics guy. The one who processed the car after Sebastian's crash."

It takes me a moment to realize what she's talking about. The accident that killed Seb's father, fifteen years ago. I was searching for information about the crash, looking for proof that Sebastian was involved. The wreck of the car itself disappeared after the initial investigation, destroyed via the police scrapyard, I assumed to cover up any evidence of Sebastian's involvement.

"Oh. Thanks," I tell her. "But... I don't need it now. I was able to expose Sebastian without it."

"Cool," Charlie gives a careless shrug. "I just wanted to make sure we had everything squared away on this one. I'm a completist like that, I can't rest until I have every last fact straight."

"I appreciate it." I tell her. "You did great work."

"See you around, sometime." Charlie says, hitching her purse. "I better get going. Places to go, people to hack,"

She leaves with a wink—back to her next job. Whoever they are, I pity them. There's nothing that escapes that woman's attention.

I envy her purpose. Getting up each morning with a new mission to fulfill. I was only launched into this madness for one reason.

*Miles.*


I collect my car from the garage and drive out to the cemetery. Nero arranged the best plot for Miles, under a shady oak tree, with a view over the ridge back towards the city. I walk through the headstones until I find it, sitting there with a polished stone, and days-old flowers wilting on the grave.

*Beloved son, brother, and friend.*

I stand there, feeling lost.

I don't know why I even came. My emotions are all over the place, a conflicting blend of guilt and regret. The grief at losing him is still there, but it's faded now, a distant whisper of that overwhelming tidal wave that urged me on all this time.

"You'd know what to do right now," I say softly to the headstone. "You always were smarter than everyone. A bitch to beat during trivia night," I add. "But we didn't hold it against you."

I take a seat on the bench nearby, wondering what Miles would say to me right now. Would he even recognize me? I'm not so sure. He knew the loyal friend, the fun hang, the Avery that was just one of the guys. He never even glimpsed the sharpest parts of me: My rage, and fury, the passion I didn't even know was lurking inside.

But Sebastian did. He saw all of me, even the darkest parts. He said he loved them, no matter what.

"Avery?"

I turn. It's Miles's mother, Debbie, approaching his grave with a fresh bouquet of flowers in her hands. "Sweetheart, look at you! Nero said you were traveling," she adds, pulling me into a fierce hug. "How was your trip? I'm so happy you're home."

"It was… Fine," I lie. I watch her change out the flowers, carefully tending to the grave. It's clear, she visits often, and she settles on the bench beside me with a sigh.

"How have you been?" I ask, immediately feeling like it's a stupid question to ask the woman while we're at her son's grave. I haven't seen her since the funeral, that awful day I barely remember for the grief and guilt.

Debbie's eyes go to the headstone for a moment before coming back to me and her smile is weary.

"I'm coping. Every day is a challenge, but I'm learning to deal with it."

I nod. What else can I do?

Her son is gone, and nothing will bring him back again.

We sit there in silence for a moment, but there's something itching at my conscience, and I can't ignore it any longer.

I turn to her. "I've wanted to tell you, I'm so sorry. For not seeing the signs... I had no idea what was going on with Miles. That he was in debt and struggling. If I'd known, I could have done something. I would have helped—"

"Shh," she cuts me off. "Avery, you can't do that to yourself. Wondering 'What if?' You think I haven't done the same thing, a thousand times?" Debbie shakes her head sadly. "I grieve my son, and I always will, but what happened was his doing. He was responsible, no one else. He could have reached out for help, talked to any one of us, but... It just didn't turn out that way."

"You don't blame me?" I ask, part-relieved, part-pained.

"I don't blame anyone," Debbie says calmly. "Not even that Wolfe guy. Miles made his own choices, and he'll be the one to answer for them."

I swallow hard. "I wish he'd made a different choice."

"Me too, sweetie. Me too."

She reaches across, and squeezes my hand, gazing at the headstone. There's something solitary in her expression that makes me feel like I'm intruding, so I politely get to my feet. "It was good seeing you," I offer.

"You too, sweetheart. You take care."

I walk slowly back through the graveyard, my thoughts spinning. It was so much easier when everything was black and white to me: Good versus evil. Miles was an angel who'd been tempted and wronged, and Sebastian was the devil who'd destroyed him.

Now, I know how wrong I was. The past months have proved to me, no one is completely good or evil. There are shades of gray. Darkness and light exist in everyone.

Even me.

And Sebastian. He's not the monster he thinks he is—or that I assumed, back when all of this began. He might have been responsible for the crash that killed his father, but he's suffered with the guilt and shame every day since. And I can't blame him for what happened to Miles, not really. Debbie was right, Miles had a hundred choices, and he picked one I'll never understand—but that was his doing, not Seb's.

And nothing I do will ever bring him back again.

My eyes sting, and I'm shocked to find tears rolling down my cheeks as I walk. I pause, sobbing there under the shade of the trees, the emotion suddenly overwhelming me. I weep with the aching loss of it all, not just Miles, and all the innocent hopes I'd been carrying for a life we could spend together. I weep for the person I could have been with him, and the man he'll never get to become. A husband, a father.

My friend.

I don't know how long I cry for him, shaking with pain and regret, but when I finally surface from my breakdown, gasping for air, I find a strange stillness has settled in my chest where the grief used to be.

I feel lighter. Freer.

Something like peace.

I exhale. "Goodbye, Miles," I whisper, feeling the last chains of my past leaving me. I know in my heart, it's time to move on.

Now, if only I could feel that way about Sebastian...

I walk back to my car, wondering if he's safe now, wherever he is. He left to protect me, I have to believe that, but we still have no idea who wanted him dead. Whoever it was, they clearly have resources and connections. Planting a bomb on that plane was no small measure, especially since they were willing to kill me too as collateral damage to get to him—

I stop suddenly, feeling a chill all the way to my bones.

*How did they know Sebastian would be on the plane?*

It was Wolfe Capital's private jet, but I was the one who was traveling back to England. Sebastian had been taken into custody by Interpol. His lawyers didn't get him out for hours, and it wasn't public knowledge. How could anyone know he would hijack the plane at the last minute to get to me?

They couldn't. It doesn't make any sense.

Which means Sebastian wasn't the target of the explosion...

It was me.

## Chapter 13

## *Avery*

"Welcome to England. Are you traveling for business or pleasure?"

"Pleasure," I reply, trying not to flinch as the border agent glances at my fake passport, up to my face, and back again.

There's a brief pause, and then he slams down the stamp. "Enjoy your stay."

But it's not the thought of a fun vacation that drives me on, moving with determination to baggage reclaim.

No, I've got unfinished business here alright. And I'm determined to get answers this time.

It didn't take me long to put the pieces together, once I realized the bomb was intended for me, not Sebastian. After all, he may have a list a mile long of people wishing him harm, but me?

Nobody cares if I live or die. I can think of only two people who have been interested in who I am, and what I'm doing: Sebastian...

And his uncle, Richard.

Looking back, it seems obvious now. He was the one who suggested I take the jet back to London. Insisted on it, even. He had a convenient excuse why he and Sebastian's mother weren't flying with me that evening, so I would be all alone in the cabin. And as the new head of Wolfe Capital, he had full access to their jet. It would have been easy for him to gain access to the hanger, and plant something on-board. Or, more likely, pay someone else to do it.

But why would he want to kill me?

That's the question that drove me back to my apartment to pack a bag, and book a flight to London, leaving ASAP. It may be crazy to fly back, *towards* the danger. I have a chance to walk away, and let Richard think his plan was a success. But something in my gut is telling me, I won't ever be able to relax until I know what the hell is going on. This story isn't over yet.

Why would he want me dead?

I'm not a threat to him. In fact, I've done everything he wanted. When I investigated the past and exposed that Sebastian was the one really driving in the accident that killed his father, I handed control of the company to Richard on a silver platter. He may have covered up the truth about the crash back when it happened, but that was to protect his investments, and the future of the family. There's no love lost between him and Sebastian, and I can only imagine how he's celebrating, now there's nothing standing in his way.

So why come after me? The truth about Sebastian was already splashed over every website and newspaper in the world.

It doesn't make any sense.

That's why I'm back here in England, to try and figure out what I've missed. I spent the flight going over every detail I've discovered on this mission: the police reports, and cover-up, looking for a clue. Charlie's tip, tracking down the forensics guy, is pretty much my only new lead, so I start there: Hailing a cab outside Arrivals, and directing him to the man's address.

It turns out to be a leafy suburb, on the outskirts of London. The house is large and set back from the road, with a lush front yard. I can hear the sound of kids playing in the back, and when I ring the doorbell, a lanky man in his fifties answers, dressed in a rumpled sweater and corduroy pants.

"Brian Kendall?" I ask. He nods. "I really need to talk to you." I say firmly. "It's about a case you worked, fifteen years ago. The death of Patrick Wolfe."

I'm braced to have to charm my way into the house. Everyone else I've talked to about the accident has wanted nothing to do with me, but Brian seems to deflate right away.

His shoulders sag. He lets out a weary sigh. "You better come in then."

I blink. "Really?"

He stands aside, beckoning me in. "I suppose a part of me has been waiting for this day," he admits, as I step inside the warmly decorated house. "Call it a sign of a guilty conscience."

"Brian, what's going on?" a female voice comes from the hallway, and I find a pleasant looking blonde woman, wiping her hands on an apron.

"This young lady needs to talk to me. About Patrick Wolfe."

Her face changes, turning nervous. "Brian, no. You don't have to talk to anybody. Just send her away."

"It's alright, Suze. Come on," he tells me. "We can talk in my study."

I follow him down a hallway lined with family pictures, of Brian with his wife and two kids. Riding lessons... The tennis club...Ski vacations and summers on the beach. I can't help wondering how a mid-level forensics guy has managed such a comfortable lifestyle.

An instinct tells me, it has something to do with his guilty conscience.

"You have a lovely home," I offer, as he shows me into a book-lined study with a small desk and a couch covered in documents and crime scene photos. He quickly clears a space to sit.

"Sorry for the mess," he apologizes. "I'm working on an appeal. I volunteer for an organization that tries to free wrongly convicted people."

"That's very virtuous of you," I remark.

He looks ashamed. "It's the least I can do."

More guilt. Just what is this guy trying to make amends for?

"Do you want to tell me what happened?" I prompt, as he paces, full of nervous energy. "I know that you were the one who examined the car, after the crash. And then it disappeared, sent to a junkyard by mistake."

"It wasn't a mistake," he says, with a heavy sigh. "I sent the paperwork through on purpose, to make sure nobody would be able to double-check my report."

"Why?" I ask, getting chilled. "I saw what you wrote. The report was clean. What did you really find?"

Brian sits behind the desk, then stands up again. "The vehicle brakes weren't functioning," he says finally, meeting my eyes. "The crash... It wasn't because of any driver error. There would have been an accident, no matter what."

"You mean... It wasn't really Sebastian's fault?" I gape. All this time, he's been thinking he killed his own father, and it turns out, it wasn't his poor driving that led to the crash. "But I don't understand," I add, processing the revelation. "Why wouldn't you tell anyone? Why would you cover up a mechanical failing?"

"Because it wasn't a failing." Brian says grimly. "The brakes had been cut."

I stare at him in disbelief. "Cut..." I echo. "But... How? Who would do something like that?"

He looks away. "I have no idea," he says, but it sounds like a lie.

"So what happened?" I demand. "Why didn't you put that in your report?"

He sighs again, looking down at his feet. "Because someone showed up at my office one night and offered me an unthinkable amount of money to cover it up."

"Who?" I ask, leaning forwards.

He pauses, then looks up to meet my eyes.

"Richard Wolfe."

Sebastian's uncle. Somehow, everything leads back to him.

"I know it was wrong, but you have to understand, my oldest son was just a boy then and he needed an expensive surgery." Brian adds urgently. "I was desperate for money already and... And I guess it was just the right time to do the wrong thing."

His voice cracks a little, and I can see that he's wracked with guilt.

"So you did it," I say, still reeling.

He nods sadly. "I took the cash, had the car scrapped, and mixed up the paperwork. I told myself it was a victimless crime. Those men were already dead, it wasn't like my report would bring them back. Nobody got charged, and... The whole thing just went away. A tragic accident. At least, it was. But then I saw the news reports last month, accusing Sebastian Wolfe of killing them. It makes me feel sick to think that the poor kid thought it was his fault this whole time."

That makes two of us.

"But you can come forward now," I tell him, my hopes rising. "You can tell the police what you know—about the report, and Richard Wolfe—"

But Brian is already shaking his head, eyes wide. "I can't. It would ruin my family. My kids don't deserve that. They shouldn't have their lives destroyed because of something I did. Besides, what's the point? The son died in that plane crash. It's all ancient history now, there's no use dragging it all up again."

I can't tell him that this new information could change everything for Sebastian.

"Do you have any proof?" I try, changing course. "Any way for me to verify what you've told me?"

He shakes his head. "I burned the original report, like Richard told me to. There's nothing left."

"Nothing but your word," I remind him.

He shakes his head. "I'm sorry, I truly am, but I won't put my family at risk."

I sigh. As much as I hate it, I can understand where he's coming from. And knowing that Richard is capable of murder…

"Thank you for your time," I offer him, and then leave—empty-handed, but with my head spinning from these new revelations.

The brakes were deliberately cut, which means someone planned to kill Sebastian's father.

Richard. His own brother. He murdered Patrick in cold blood. Out of what, jealousy, that he'd built a billion-dollar business and a happy family, while Richard's own career stumbled?

Now, the way Richard moved in and took up with Sebastian's mother makes a twisted kind of sense. He wanted to replace Patrick—in every way.

I think back over everything I've learned, and it all clicks into place. When he stepped in, and organized a cover-up after the accident, it wasn't to protect Sebastian the way we all thought… It was to make sure his own crimes stayed hidden, forever.

And then once I publicly accused Sebastian, Richard had the bomb planted on the jet, to make sure I would never go digging any further.

I was just another loose end to him.

But what do I do now?

I need to find Sebastian. He has to know what really happened—and what Richard is capable of.

But he's a ghost now. Disappeared, leaving no trace behind.

How can I possibly I contact him?

I puzzle over it all the way back into London. I check into a luxurious, low-key hotel off Bond Street, and wrack my brain for a way to reach Sebastian. He wouldn't have told his family where he was going, and he doesn't have many close friends—

Except there is someone I know Sebastian trusts more than anyone.

Enough to share me with him, during our filthy, illicit threesome.

Anthony St. Clair. Saint. His buddy from Oxford.

And I know just where I can find him.

I change into a chic black dress, and catch a car across the city, to the discreet club where Sebastian took me. It feels like a lifetime ago now, the way I followed him inside, full of anticipation and desire.

Now, I march calmly to the door, with a very different mission in mind. Sebastian said that Saint hangs out here often. I figure if I don't see him, there'll be someone who knows where he might be.

"Excuse me?" The woman minding the front desk steps to block my way. "Are you a member here?"

*Shit.*

"Umm, no…"

"Then I'm afraid I can't give you access," she says crisply. "This is a private establishment."

Damn. I think fast.

"Oh my gosh, I'm such an idiot," I blurt, acting flustered. "I'm supposed to be meeting this guy here, and I don't even have his number, we met at the gym, but... His name is Saint," I add, dropping my voice. "He's like... a duke or something! So hot. I'm running late, so he's probably already inside...?"

The woman gives a little eyeroll. "Mr. St Clair. Of course," she sighs, stepping aside. "He doesn't seem to know the meaning of the word 'private,'" she adds. "He's in the lounge."

"Thank you!" I trill, breezing past her, and into the dim, sensual surroundings of the club.

It's still early, but there are a few people here already: Glamorous couples relaxing in the plush booths, people flirting for the night ahead. I'm not surprised to see a naked woman sandwiched between two men in the corner, her head already tipped back in pleasure; lips parted as they share her body between their capable hands.

It's not so long ago that *I* was that woman... Discovering the ultimate pleasure right here under Sebastian's expert tutelage, pushed beyond every limit and boundary to the sheer heady bliss of release.

I feel a pang of longing—not just for that pleasure, but for Sebastian's embrace. The way he seemed to know my every fantasy, the ones I'd never even admitted out loud.

The sexual bond between us was like nothing else. And the prospect of life without it...?

Unthinkable.

I square my shoulders, and move deeper into the club, determined to track him down again, no matter what. Then I see exactly who's going to help me: his friend, Saint, all six-foot-two of his louche, dark-haired frame. He's lingering near the bar, flirting with a woman in a gorgeous diamond necklace...

And nothing else.

"Saint," I say, sliding in beside them.

I give the woman a look, and she tactfully disappears, as Saint practically chokes on his drink. "Avery?" he says, looking shocked to see me. "What are you doing here....? I mean, what a miracle," he covers quickly. "We all thought you were dead."

"Nice try," I smirk. He's already given the game away: He's more surprised to see me in the club, alone, than the fact that I'm alive and kicking, which means he's already connected with Sebastian.

He knows we didn't die in that crash.

"I'm looking for Sebastian," I tell him bluntly.

"According to the papers, he's sadly passed from this mortal coil," Saint replies, recovering his usual nonchalant demeanor. "Pity, the man knew how to spice things up."

"Cut the bullshit," I lean closer. "This is important. I need to speak to him."

"And, just supposing he was alive and well, what makes you think I would know where he is?" Saint arches an eyebrow.

"You're his best friend. If anyone knows, it's you."

"I'm sorry to disappoint," Saint says, knocking back the rest of his drink. "I'm not the man's keeper. In fact, I've got a busy schedule all on my own. Places to go, people to fuck, you know how it is," he winks. "But if you're lonely and looking for some company tonight, I have a date waiting in a group room. You're more than welcome to join us," he adds, with a suggestive smirk. "We can continue where we left off..."

He trails his fingertips over my bare arm. I flinch. "Tell Sebastian, he has to contact me," I say urgently, but he just smiles.

"Suit yourself."

Saint saunters off, beckoning the naked woman back to him with a snap of his fingers before they stroll from the room.

I watch him go, frustrated. He knows something, and I don't have time for these games. Richard is still out there, and who knows what else he might be planning?

I have to get to Sebastian, wherever he's hiding.

I leave the club, and call Charlie, back in the States. It's the middle of the night there, but she answers immediately, sounding fresh and alert.

"What do you need?"

I smile. No need for small talk here. "Anthony St Clair, he's a guy here in London. I need to know if he has any travel listed, or unusual expenses lately."

I'm expecting her to have to call me back later, but instead, Charlie barely pauses for breath.

"Oh, yeah, I see the guy..." she says, and I hear the tap of computer keys. "Fancy bastard. Has a thing for expensive wine and antique books," she muses, "At least, according to his credit card bills."

I don't ask how she's looking at them right now. Not when this information is exactly what I need. "Anything else?" I ask eagerly. "An apartment rental, or plane tickets. Something out of his usual routine."

"Ah, here it is," Charlie says. "He's booked on a flight to Venice in the morning. And it looks like he's been paying for a rental apartment there for the past week."

"That's it!" I exclaim, excited. "I knew it."

It has to be Sebastian.

"Can you send me the rental address?" I ask, stepping out in the street to hail a cab. If Saint thinks he can hide Sebastian away, he's got another thing coming.

Next stop: Venice.

## Chapter 14

## *Sebastian*

Venice. The city of love. I should have picked a better place to wait for my forger to be done, but who am I kidding?

There's not a place I could go in the world that wouldn't make me think of her.

*Avery...*

I pace the small apartment, feeling like a caged animal. Her face haunts my every waking moment—and at night, she fills my dreams. Where is she now? I wonder obsessively. Is she out there cursing my name for leaving her, or does she understand by now, that it was the only way?

Dammit.

I don't like to think of her off somewhere, without me. Waking up alone. Going about her day. Slipping between the sheets at night in an empty bed.

Or even worse, with company.

Fuck. No. I can't think that way. I'll tear this whole damn place apart. I look around, needing a distraction. It's a comfortable vacation rental—Saint set it up for me—with stylish antiques and Italian décor, but right now, it feels like I'm trapped in purgatory: the waiting room between heaven and hell.

The heaven of my life with her. The hell of a world where she isn't by my side.

*Are you sure there isn't a way...?*

The whispers of doubt rise up, taunting me, so I grab a coat and head out, losing myself in the bustle of crowded streets and picturesque canals. I should be laying low in case anyone recognizes me, but I can't stay cooped up there with my own thoughts a moment longer.

She's safer without me.

I repeat the mantra as I pace the cobblestones, telling myself that I have no choice. Someone was willing to blow up that jet to get to me, which means Avery can never know peace with me in her life. The sooner we both put our twisted love affair behind us and move on, the better. Once my papers are back, I can disappear forever: It's not just a simple passport I'm waiting on, but a whole new identity crafted by the best black-market forgers around, with an online trail and paper dupes planted in government offices around the world that will never be questioned. Sebastian Wolfe will cease to exist, leaving nothing but headlines and dark scandal in his wake.

I'll be free. Reborn. But until then, I have nothing left to do but wait.

Wait, and go mad with wanting her.

I walk for hours, lost in the hum of the city and my own dark thoughts, until a text comes through from Saint that he's arrived. I'm in no hurry to be cooped up in the flat again, so I suggest meeting at a discreet restaurant nearby. When I arrive, the place is packed with the late-night crowds: Waitresses darting around with trays in their hands and so many customers talking that it all blends into a buzz of sound. I spot Saint sitting in the back in a corner booth. I make my way over, and he greets me with a hug, and a slap on my back.

"Good to see you," I say, meaning it. There's not a single other person I would dream of reaching out to at a time like this, but Saint came through for me without a word of hesitation.

But plenty of wry jokes.

"I can't say the same about you," he cracks, waving the waitress over and ordering a bottle of wine and enough food to feed an army. "You look like hell, mate. Anyone would think you'd died."

I roll my eyes at his quips. "Funnily enough, fleeing for your life takes a toll on a man."

"Psh," Saint says with a grin. "Don't ruin the illusion. I thought life would be one big adventure when you're a man on the run."

"Sure," I respond dryly. "It's round-the-clock excitement here."

"Well, at least you picked a spot with decent amenities," Saint says, admiring the food—and the waitress who brings plates of bread and tartare to the table. "Can't be too bad, being holed up here."

I give a shrug. "I'll sleep easier once I have my new papers and put some distance between me and Sebastian Wolfe. Literally," I say. I've been thinking of South America for a while: Colombia maybe, and Brazil. Places oceans away where nobody would think to find me.

Places where I could get lost.

I reach for the bread, and I've just taken a bite when Saint says casually, "You know, Avery came to see me."

My head snaps up. "Avery?" I repeat, my pulse suddenly

pounding. "She's in London? What? Why?"

"Why do you think?" Saint gives me a look. "She's searching for you."

*Shit.*

I can't deny the way my heart leaps at the thought that she still wants to be with me, but that brief relief is drowned out by the danger that she's putting herself in.

"What happened?" I demand. "Tell me everything."

Saint shrugs and sips his wine. "Nothing much to tell. She came to find me at the club, and demanded I reveal your location."

"Did you tell her anything?" I ask, gripped.

"Of course not!" Saint protests. "I'm the height of discretion. Like James Bond, but better looking."

I exhale. "Good," I say grimly. "She can't ever know where I am."

Saint pauses, giving me a look of scrutiny. "Are you really so sure about that? You have the money and the resources to go anywhere and do anything. If you're going to disappear, then why not take her with you?"

I shake my head. "I can't. She wouldn't be safe."

"Is that true?" he counters. "Or just a convenient excuse, not to follow through on anything, and make the relationship work."

I scowl. "You think I haven't gone over this a hundred times?" I tell him angrily. "Looking for some way we could be together? But there's no other way. This is the plan now. There's nothing left to say."

"That's too bad."

A voice behind us makes me startle. I turn, my jaw dropping in disbelief as Avery herself saunters over, slides into the booth, and fixes me with a cool, demanding stare.

"I guess plans change."

## Chapter 15

### *Avery*

"Avery..."

Sebastian stares at me across the table, dumbstruck. He wasn't expecting me, that much is clear.

Saint looks back and forth between us, and tactfully clears his throat. "You know, this seems like a good time for me to step out and make a phone call."

He slips out of the booth and disappears, leaving us alone.

I reach over and take a piece of the fresh-baked bread, savoring the taste of it. "Well, I have to give you points for hiding out somewhere with great food," I remark, casual. "Even if you did break my heart and abandon me to do it."

Sebastian's jaw tenses. He looks good, too good, even with dark shadows under his eyes and a look of haunted fury in his eyes, and everything in me aches to hold him again.

"You shouldn't be here," he grinds out between gritted teeth. "You're supposed to be back in America. Anywhere but here."

"I need to talk to you. It's important," I add, but Sebastian is already on his feet.

"There's nothing left to say between us. I thought I made that clear when I left."

"Right," I glare at the memory. "Thanks for that, by the way. There's nothing a girl loves more than waking up alone with a note on the pillow. Really makes her feel special. Like a high-class whore."

Regret flashes on Sebastian's face, but it's soon replaced with steely determination.

"I gave you a chance to be happy, to return to your real life. You'll be safe there."

"So, that's why you left," I give out a bitter laugh. "All in some misguided attempt to protect me."

"Misguided?" he snaps. "Have you forgotten the plane crash? The explosion?"

"That's why I came to find you." I say urgently, taking his arm. "I need to tell you something. I've figured it all out—"

But before I can reveal what I've found about Richard and the crash, Sebastian wrenches away and walks right out of the restaurant.

*Dammit.*

I bolt up and start after him, nearly bumping into a waitress that was heading to our table in my haste. I mumble an apology and rush out the door just in time to see Sebastian disappear into the crowds.

"Seb—" I start to call after him before realizing, I can't. nobody can know who we are, not when the world still thinks we're dead. *Fuck.* I yank a hat from my purse and pull it low over my eyes as I weave through the throngs of tourists out for a late-night stroll, eyes peeled for his familiar frame.

There.

I see Sebastian turn off the main path, crossing beneath one of the narrow bridges that stretch over the canal. I speed up, drawing level in the shadows beside the water.

"Wait!" I demand, pulling him around to face me. "You have to listen to me!"

"And you need to accept that it's over!"

Sebastian's words cut me, and so does the cold look in his eyes, but this isn't about my heart. It matters more than how I feel.

"You don't understand," I tell him stubbornly, holding onto him. "This isn't about us. It's you. You didn't kill your father!"

Sebastian reels back. "What are you talking about" he demands, looking furious.

"It wasn't you," I insist again. "It's not your fault. It was Richard!"

My voice rings out, echoing off the water. Luckily, we're alone in the shadows, but as Sebastian stares at me, slack-jawed, a gondola glides closer, packed with a laughing group of tourists.

He suddenly snaps back and grabs my arm. "We have to go," he says, dragging me on, back to the main street, and down another alleyway until we arrive at a quaint building tucked beside the canal. Sebastian unlocks the door, and practically shoves me inside, looking around behind us before slamming it shut.

I follow him up to the apartment on the second floor, where he paces, trying to process what I've just said.

"Talk," he orders, still every inch the dominating presence. "It was Richard? What the hell do you mean?"

"I talked to the forensics guy," I explain, my heart in my throat. "He's the one who examined the car, after the accident. He says that the brakes had been cut. It wasn't an accident, Sebastian. It wouldn't have mattered who was driving, there was no way to control the car."

Sebastian stares at me, a thousand emotions conflicting in his gaze.

"No..." he whispers, sagging back.

"Yes."

I explain it all to him, everything I learned from my visit with Brian, and my own conclusions about Richard and the explosion on the jet. "It wasn't meant for you, Sebastian," I insist, pacing in the small, luxurious room. "Richard was trying to kill me, to tie up any loose ends. He knew I'd been digging around in the past, and he couldn't risk me uncovering anything more about what happened."

Sebastian takes a deep breath, and I can see his mind ticking over, as brilliant as always. "So why did you?" he asks, finally meeting my gaze.

"What?" I pause, confused.

"Keep digging." He takes a step closer to me. "I left you. It was over. You could have been free. Free of me, away from all of this shit for good. So why did you come back and keep investigating?" he demands. "I don't understand."

I swallow hard.

"I love you," I whisper it, then say it again, stronger this time. "I love you, Sebastian. I've always loved you, even when I tried to hate you. And I'm not willing to live without you."

Confessing my feelings makes me feel like a weight has lifted off my shoulders. It's a truth that I've tried to deny to myself for a long time, but the feeling is too powerful. I can't deny it, and if I'm honest with myself, I don't want to anymore.

"Avery..."

Sebastian whispers my name, almost like a prayer on his lips. The agony in his eyes turns to something like wonder, and then he's closing the distance between us, and pulling me into his arms.

Yes.

I melt against him as his lips claim mine in a heart-stopping kiss. *Here.* This is where I'm meant to be. With him, no matter what.

*Forever.*

Sebastian groans against my mouth. "Fuck, baby, I've missed you so much…"

"Me too," I gasp, already arching closer, wanting to feel every inch of him. The touch of his skin has unleashed something inside of me, something desperate and wanting. I draw back, panting. "Please, Sebastian… I need you. *Now.*"

With a growl, he grabs me by the hips and lifts me, slamming me back against the wall. I moan, pressing against him, loving the possessive squeeze of his grip and the sharp nip of his teeth against my neck as he blazes a trail of kisses down to my collarbone. His hands are everywhere, roaming and squeezing, and mine are doing just the same. I tear his shirt open, feasting on his salty skin.

Mine. All mine.

My hands go to his fly, fumbling with my breathless need, and Sebastian helps me, tearing it open and shoving down his jeans and briefs to free his cock, already stiff and bucking against my hands.

Then, he's parting my thighs wider, hiking up my skirt and yanking my panties aside.

"I can't hold back," he growls, claiming my mouth again with a fevered kiss.

"Good," I moan, impatient. "Don't. Don't stop for anything."

He thrusts inside with one savage thrust.

"Fuck…"

We both groan from the illicit pleasure, his thick girth sinking deep, stretching me wide open in the way only he can do. "Seb!" I cry out, throwing my head back as he grips me tighter, pistoning deeper and grinding up inside me, just right. "Oh God... More... *Seb*!"

My scream echoes as he slams into me again, and again, pounding me open in a dizzying rhythm that leaves me sobbing in his arms. I hold on for dear life, in ecstasy, feeling filled for the first time since he left me.

Feeling complete.

"My sparrow..." Sebastian groans, his eyes blazing with pleasure as he grinds deeper, pinning me to the wall with the force of his thrusts. "Fuck, there's nothing like you. Like this tight cunt."

"But you left me," I sob, still angry despite the pleasure. "You fucking walked away."

"I know," Sebastian gasps a ragged breath. "I thought I was protecting you... I wanted you to be free."

"Don't you dare try that shit again," I manage, even as I'm on the brink of insanity. I lever against his shoulders, bouncing on his cock. "Don't you ever leave me."

"Never." Sebastian vows. His thrusts still, and he holds me there in his arms, eyes dark on mine. "I swear it, baby," he says, filling me so perfectly. Surrounding me. Owning me. "I'll never leave you again."

He rocks into me slowly, eyes still fixed on mine, and fuck. It's too good. Too perfect. I can't hold back. My orgasm sweeps through me, a blissful rush of sweet release. I cry out, calling his name, sobbing against him as my body writhes, and Sebastian comes with a raw, animal cry.

*Forever.*

I hold him, gasping, as the pleasure floods through me, and I know, it's the truth. I wouldn't let him go again, even if he tried.

We're in this together now, no matter what.

# Chapter 16

## *Avery*

I wake the next morning to the warm glow of Italian sunrise... And Sebastian sprawled beside me in bed, his arms flung protectively around me.

I sigh, feeling a wash of contentment, a kind of peace that's eluded me ever since we parted.

*This is exactly where I belong.*

The sense of security lulls me back to sleep again, there in his arms, and when I wake again, it's later: The sun higher in the sky outside the balcony, and the sound of the shower running, the bed empty beside me.

I sit up, yawning, feeling the pleasant ache in my limbs. Our frantic reunion comes flooding back to me, the slide of Sebastian's body on mine, the sweet friction of his cock, stretching me open...

"Good morning," Sebastian steps out of the bathroom, naked and glistening from the shower with a tiny towel wrapped around his waist. He pauses there in the doorway, watching me with a smile.

I beam back. "It is, isn't it?"

I know we have a world of drama and danger still to figure out, but right now, just being back together is enough for me.

Sebastian sees my appreciative stare, lingering on his body. He gives a chuckle, and his stride is more of a swagger as he crosses to the bed. Leaning over, he presses a sizzling kiss to my lips. "Hungry?" he murmurs, as I reach up and pull him closer.

"That depends…" I savor the taste of him, his scent so fresh and clean. "Would I need to leave this bed to get my fill?"

Sebastian's eyebrow arches in amusement. "She needs filling, hmmm?" He trails a hand over my curves, teasing with a featherlight touch. "We'll have to take care of that."

"Yes." I nod eagerly. "Soon. Right away."

There's a sudden knock at the door. Sebastian pulls back, and I let out a groan of frustration.

He laughs. "Hold that thought," he says with a wink, before going to answer the door. I hear voices in the hallway, and a moment later, he returns with some bakery bags.

"And voilà," he announces, presenting them with a grin.

I tear one open, and gasp happily when I find an assortment of pastries. "Breakfast?"

"From a bakery down the street. Try the lemon one," he says, lifting the delicate shell-shaped pastry to my lips. "You'll love it."

I do. The sweet cream pastries—and this new lightness in Sebastian's smile. He seems like a weight has been lifted from his shoulders; the dark shadows are gone from his gaze, and instead, there's an almost boyish gleam of excitement as he wolfs down a pastry in one single bite.

I giggle, pretending to bat his hands away. "Leave some for me!" I protest, laughing.

He grins, snatching another. "Think fast!"

He grabs the bags, and opens the doors out to the balcony, where a small table and chairs are set, overlooking the early-morning canal. I grab a robe, and follow him, settling at the table to enjoy the view.

Of him.

"What is it?" Sebastian asks, seeing me looking.

I flush. "Nothing," I reply. "I just... I guess a part of me thought I'd never see you again. That you would disappear, and I would never be able to track you down."

Sebastian reaches across the table and takes my hand. "I thought about it. I wanted to," he admits, "Not to leave you, but to protect you. But... I guess a part of me wasn't ready to give up on you either. It's probably why I'm still here."

"Why did you wait?" I ask. "That's one thing I still don't understand. You could have had papers done in a matter of days. You got that passport for me quickly enough."

Sebastian gives a rueful grin. "So quickly, the guy spooked, and refused to make another for me. I had to find new forgers, and have new bank accounts set up in another name... But the truth is, I wasn't ready to go just yet. I suppose I was hoping you'd come."

"It would have been easier if you'd just left a forwarding address," I quip, taking another bite of pastry. "Although Saint practically handed it to me on a silver platter."

Sebastian snorts. "So much for subterfuge. The guy has no game."

"But he is good at making himself scarce," I say with a smile. He texted us late last night to say he'd met a new friend and was traveling with her now.

An attractive, female friend, no doubt.

"So, what's the plan now?" I ask, with a reluctant sigh. As much as I want to pretend that I'm here with Sebastian on some romantic getaway, there's no avoiding the truth. I brace myself for the answer, but instead, Sebastian's smile stays mischievous.

"Well, as far as I see it, there's only one thing we can do here in Venice." He pauses, and takes another bite of food for dramatic effect before announcing: "Sightseeing."

I blink in surprise. "What, really?"

He smiles. "I'm still waiting on the papers for my new identity. They should be ready tonight, but until then, we might as well make the most of our time here. It is the city of love, after all," he adds, taking my hand. "Don't you want to explore?"

A part of me still wants to drag Sebastian back to bed and spend the day making up for lost time, but then a gondola glides past below us, and I see the city coming to life, the light reflecting beautifully off the canal.

I feel a flicker of excitement. After all the heartbreak and grief of the past week, getting to spend the day like a carefree tourist seems like a gift. A chance we can't pass up.

"I'd love to," I say finally, giving him a happy smile. "Let's go."

"But not just yet," Sebastian adds, giving me a smoldering grin. "I'm still hungry."

"For more food?" I tease, flirty.

He shakes his head, and then in a single motion, he gets to his feet, picks me up over his shoulder, and takes me back to bed to show me exactly what he's got in mind.

It's another couple of hours before we drag ourselves out of bed. After Sebastian insists on helping soap every inch of me down in the shower, we finally dress and make it out into the city to explore. We're dressed down, like regular tourists, and I even find an 'I heart Venice' T-shirt and baseball hat for Sebastian to wear, while I hide behind massive sunglasses and a big floppy sunhat.

Stylish, no. Discreet? I'm hoping. There's no reason for

anyone to give us a second glance, and we soon blend into the crowds, strolling in no particular direction as Sebastian shows me what he's learned about the city since hiding out here.

I'm in heaven. We visit St. Mark's Basilica, marveling at the beauty of the gold mosaics and altar. We visit artisans' shops and a gorgeous opera house. We even go to a food market, browsing the bustling aisles and tasting the fresh oils and local delicacies.

The whole time, I can't stop looking at Sebastian, loving the side of him that I'm seeing. He's happier than I've ever seen him. His smile comes easily, and when we're taking a touristy ride on a gondola, he exchanges jokes in Italian with the driver. I don't understand what they're saying, but the way they both laugh makes my own heart feel lighter.

I hope to God that this isn't just temporary. That somehow, we can find a way to be this happy together into the future, even if that seems impossible right now.

I shake off the thoughts of the future, I pledged to ignore them for the day, and find that we're strolling on a narrow cobblestone street of designer stores and boutiques. My eyes land on a chic little window, decorated with exquisite lingerie pieces in the finest silks.

Sebastian notices my stare. "Let's go in," he suggests, then takes my hand and leads us in to the tiny jewel box of a store, all plush velvet and glittering chandeliers.

An assistant materializes, an older woman with perfect red lipstick. "And what are we browsing for today?" she asks, immediately friendly.

Clearly, all the tourist outfits in the world can't disguise Sebastian's natural charisma and power.

"What do you think?" Sebastian asks me, a suggestive smile playing on the edge of his lips.

I smile back. "Why don't you choose?"

His grin spreads. "Perfect. We'll try that… and that… and of course, those…" he points out some of the gorgeous pieces, and the woman leaps to attend to us.

"Excellent choices. Please, come this way."

By the time she leads us to the dressing room, tucked away at the back of the store, there's a pile of lace and silk waiting for me. Sebastian plants himself on a wingback chair right outside the room.

"Start with the emerald green set," he tells me, a flash of dominance in his gaze. "Show me how it fits, I want to see everything."

I feel a shiver of excitement. "Yes, sir," I reply with a smirk, and then pull the curtain closed as I strip down and try on the first outfit.

Well, outfit is a stretch. The bra is barely a whisper of silk, and the panties tie over each hip in an eruption of tiny ribbons.

"Seb?" I call, a little hesitant at my revealing reflection.

"Open up."

His voice is firm and triggers that gorgeous warmth inside me. *Wanting to please him.* I suck in a breath, and ease the curtain open.

"Well?" I ask, awkwardly presenting myself. "What do you think?"

Sebastian's eyes darken, as he lounges there in his seat. "Don't be modest," he says, beckoning to me. "Turn around. Show me everything."

My pulse kicks. I can hear the murmurs of voices out in the shop, just a few feet away, but suddenly, it feels like we're totally alone.

Hidden, and intimate.

I do as Sebastian says, slowly pivoting up on my tiptoes, displaying myself to him in the luxurious underwear.

He lets out a hiss of satisfaction. "That's right. See how pretty you are, baby?"

He rises, turning me to look at my reflection in the mirror, as he takes position behind me.

"See how you deserve to be worshipped..." His hand goes to my shoulder, his fingertips barley grazing my skin as he straightens the twisted strap of the bra. "Every part of you..." His hand skims lower, over the full swell of my breast. Sebastian dips his head to kiss the bare curve of my shoulder as his hands move over me. "Every last inch."

I shudder under his touch, pleasure spiraling out.

He's so close that I can feel his body heat radiating into me. His searing gaze is fixed on my reflection: The reflection of the both of us, his hands still softly stroking over me.

"I think it's perfect," he replies, his voice thick. "You're perfect."

He kisses my neck again, as his fingertips come together, plucking my nipple in a tight pinch. I moan in surprise, and Sebastian is quick to press a hand over my mouth, muffling me.

"Shh, baby," he groans against me. "Don't make a sound. Don't let anyone know how wet you're getting."

*Oh God.*

Sebastian nudges me back into the dressing room and yanks the curtain shut behind us before pulling me back against his body. My head falls back against his shoulder, my heart pounding as his hands continue their filthy exploration of my every curve and slope.

He's driving me crazy.

"Seb..." I gasp breathlessly. I turn in his arms, wrapping my arms around his neck as I find his lips and pull him into a fevered kiss. I arch against him, feeling the thick ridge of his erection in his pants, and God, it only turns me on more. I rub against him, eager, but he moves back, out of reach.

"Not now, baby," Sebastian insists, even though I can see the lust in his eyes.

"No?" I pout, reaching for the ribbons on the panties. "Oh, well, I better try on the next outfit them."

I tug them free, letting the silk fall in a heap on the floor.

Sebastian stifles a groan. "Naughty girl," he scolds me, as I shimmy out of the bra, too, leaving me naked in front of him.

"I'm just following your instructions," I reply lightly, "You said to show you *everything*."

Sebastian's eyes flash, but his jaw tightens with self-control. "I'm not touching you yet, Sparrow. Not here. I have plans for us. Later."

The thought fills me with anticipation, but I love tormenting him like this, too.

"Pity," I give a sigh, sinking back against the wall. I slide my hand over my naked body, down between my legs. "But you're right. I'm already wet. And if you won't touch me..." I whisper, boldly. "I'll just have to touch myself."

I ease my fingers against my wet heat, and give a little mewl of pleasure.

In an instant, Sebastian has me up against the wall with his hand pressed over my mouth, muffling me. "I told you to be quiet," he grounds out, but every word is ragged.

"So make me," I whisper, slowly rubbing my pussy. Loving this thrill, pushing his control to the brink. "Keep me quiet while I get myself off."

"Fuck, Avery..." Sebastian groans, and I smile back at him, feeling wild and wicked. "Go on then," he urges me, his mouth by my ear. "Rub that sweet clit until you break, baby. But just know, I won't go easy on you later. I'll make you beg for your release."

"Yes..." I moan into his palm, turned on like crazy. I rub myself in swift strokes, already so close to the edge.

"I should have you on your damn knees for this," Sebastian growls. "Spank that peach of an ass for your disobedience. Make you howl for mercy, so loud they all come to see what's making a fuss. You'd like that, wouldn't you?" he adds, drawing back so I can see the glitter of dark promise in his gaze. "The whole store watching you take your punishment, until I finally fuck the sass right out of you."

*Fuck.*

My vision clouds as my orgasm sweeps through me, hard and sweep. I come against my own hand, gasping.

Sebastian steps away. "Put your clothes on," he tells me with a smirk. "I'll go pay."

"For what?" I ask, still reeling.

"For everything."

We emerge from the boutique laden with bags, which I'm pretty sure is Sebastian's way of apologizing for the scene we just made. My cheeks are burning, but God, I love the feeling still thick in my veins: the intoxication of his commandments, and all our sexy fun. "Back to the apartment?" I ask him breathlessly, eager for all those plans he promised.

Sebastian nods, but once we get back, he still doesn't touch me: He just picks out lingerie and an inky silk dress for me to wear, and orders me to dress for dinner.

I slip into the clothes, my anticipation building. "Where are we going?" I ask, fastening my platform sandals, and applying a layer of scarlet lipstick.

"It's not far," Sebastian replies. He's dressed in a button-down and dress pants, with a jacket slung over his shoulder, and although I know it's a risk to go out like this, I can't help it. He looks too good to resist. "You'll like it," he adds with a cryptic smile. "I promise."

I'd like anything he has planned, but when we descend a short flight of stairs from the street, and step into the restaurant, I sound a small cry of excitement. It's a chic little jazz club, all plush booths and well-dressed diners. The trio on stage is deep into the music, and the whole place is filled with a melodic buzz. "I love it!" I exclaim, looking around. "How did you find it?"

"It's a hidden gem," he replies, guiding me into the room. "Locals only."

"Thank you," I beam at him, but his gaze is hungry on mine.

"Do you know how delicious you look?" he whispers in my ear as we move to our table. "Every man in this place wishes he was me. Hell, probably half the women too."

"Too bad for them," I whisper back, feeling a glow of power. "You're the only one who's fucking me tonight."

Sebastian's curse of desire is cut off by the waiter, who chatters away in Italian. Sebastian replies as we take a seat, his hand coming to rest under the table on my bare thigh.

"... Does that sound good to you?"

I blink. Sebastian is looking at me with private amusement, as beneath the table, his fingers trace a dizzying circle on my inner thigh.

"I... Yes. Great!" I blurt.

The waiter pours us some wine, and departs, and Sebastian sits back, enjoying the room.

And the way he's driving me crazy under the tablecloth with his hidden touch.

His fingertips lazily trace higher, barely brushing the apex of my thighs before skimming back down to my knee again.

I shudder with want. "I can't focus with you doing that," I warn him, clenching in my new panties.

"Sure you can," Sebastian smirks. "You wanted me to touch you, remember? So, I'm giving you exactly what you need."

"Bastard," I mutter, but I'm smiling at the same time.

"That's my girl." Sebastian smiles back. "Just relax and enjoy the show."

I take a deep breath, trying to control my racing desire, but it doesn't stop with the drinks. Our food arrives, and his hand stays beneath the table, relentless, teasing me into a silent frenzy as he skims my thighs… The backs of my knees… Even brushing so tantalizingly close to my pussy from time to time, until I'm practically panting for him.

Despite my haze of lust, it's a delicious dinner, and the music is amazing. There's a man sitting behind a piano, singing in a deep voice. It's a relaxed atmosphere, but undeniably romantic, the low lighting setting the mood.

The man comes to the end of a song and rises from the piano. "Thank you," he says, to the sound of applause. "Tonight, we have a very special guest joining us. Please welcome her, Miss Amelie Michaels."

He points, and a spotlight lands on our table.

Wait…

Amelie. That's the name I've been travelling under.

I turn to stare at Sebastian with wide eyes. "What did you do?" I hiss, as the crowd applauds encouragingly.

He smiles. "I want you to sing for me."

"I can do that at the apartment," I protest, flustered. Never mind the fact he's spent the past half-hour turning me on, now the whole room is looking at us. "But here… All these people watching? I can't!"

"Yes, you can," Sebastian says calmly. "And if you don't believe you can do it… Do it for me. I want to see you light up that stage, just one song. For me. Please?"

I gulp. My stomach is flip-flopping with nerves, but I could never deny him anything he wants from me...

Not when a small part of me wants it too.

"You better make it up to me," I warn him playfully, getting to my feet. My legs are unsteady, and it takes me a moment to gather my courage before walking over to the stage, my heartbeat pounding so hard that I'm sure everyone can hear it.

All eyes are on me.

*Shit.*

I take my place at the piano with the bright stage lights shining down on me, and I try not to panic. I haven't performed in public... Well, ever. And now, feeling everyone staring expectantly, I remember why.

*Sing just for him,* I tell myself. Pretend like there's nobody else in the room.

That part is simple. When Sebastian's around, everything else disappears, so I look up, finding him in the crowd. He gives me an encouraging smile, so I move my hands to the keys, and find myself playing a familiar refrain.

I played it for him once before, what feels like a lifetime ago. Back then, the words were tinted with fear and longing, but now, all that's behind us.

I open my mouth and start to sing. It's a sultry love song and as the words pour out of me, they're for him. The nerves fade away because it doesn't feel like there's anyone else in the club. It's just the two us.

Only him. Always.

Soon enough, I lose myself in the music, closing my eyes as I belt the final words. There's a long silence, as I slowly come back to the present. Then the room bursts into applause.

Holy shit!

A rush of exhilaration crashes through me, taking in the sound of their approval, and the smiling faces all around.

I did it. I really did it.

I slowly get up. Sebastian is on his feet, cheering me on as I make my way across the club and arrive back at the table. I'm blushing like crazy, but it feels amazing. "Well?" I ask, even though his reaction is written all over his face.

Sebastian pulls me in, and answers me with a hot, deep kiss. There's laughter around us, and I realize, we're not alone.

"Seb," I protest laughing, pulling back. "We still have an audience."

"Not for long."

Dropping a wad of cash on the table, he takes my hand and pulls me determinedly out of the club. "I can't believe I just did that!" I gasp, as we exit to the dark streets. "Oh my god, I've never performed in front of anyone before."

"You were incredible," Sebastian pulls me on, faster, through the late-night crowds. "Fuck, the sight of you up there... You're so beautiful."

He suddenly pulls me into a heated kiss, and I moan as his mouth finds mine, searching and insistent.

I'm flying on adrenaline, and the touch of his body is like a flame to my short fuse.

"Seb," I gasp, clawing at his shirt, dizzy with lust for him right there in the middle of the street. "I *need* you."

He groans. "I need you too, baby. Fuck..." He looks around us, then suddenly yanks me off the main street, into a dark and narrow alleyway.

"What are you—"

I don't get to finish my question before he's consuming me, his tongue in my mouth and his hands up my dress. I moan into his mouth, just as ravenous, pressing into his hands as he rips my panties aside and sinks two fingers into my wetness.

"Seb..." I moan in delight, clenching around him. "Oh God, yes."

He thrusts into me, once, twice, then pulls back with a wicked gleam in his eyes. "I need to taste you, sweetheart," he growls, already sinking to his knees. "You're so wet for me. Let me lick up every sweet drop."

My heart leaps as he grips my thighs, parting me right there in the alleyway. Some part of my brain registers that we're out in the open near the busy main street. Anyone could glance this way and see us in the shadows.

Anyone could watch him eat me out.

I shudder with hot lust, tangling my hands in his hair as Sebastian licks up against me in one incredible swoop.

"Oh God!"

I cry out as his tongue finds my sensitive nub, lapping and toying with me, sending pleasure rocking through my body. "*Seb!*" I cry, not caring who could hear us. I'm past caring now. Beyond everything but the hot slide of his tongue and the deep, thick thrust of his fingers, angling inside me to rub in time with his laps.

"That's right, Sparrow," Sebastian growls against me, pumping faster. "Tell the world who makes this pussy so tight."

He closes his lips around my clit, and sucks. Hard.

Fuck.

I come with a scream, pleasure crashing through me in intense waves. I'm breathless, soaring, but Sebastian's not done yet.

He's on his feet again in an instant, spinning me to face the wall. "Hands up, baby," he orders me harshly, shoving me face-first against the brick. "Spread wider for me. That's right. Time to take what you came here for."

I'm still reeling with my climax when I hear the sound of Sebastian's zipper. Then he grips my hips, pulls me back, and slams into me with a thick, determined stroke.

I let out a strangled cry of relief and pleasure, feeling his cock spear me wide open. Oh God, I've wanted this all night. Needed him, filling me like this.

"Seb," I chant, thrusting back to take him deeper.

"You want more, baby?" he demands harshly, his hand tangling in my hair and pulling my head back as he starts to ride me.

"Yes!"

"You need this cock, you need to take it."

"Yes!"

I'm sobbing and mindless now as he pounds into me, loving every second of the rough fuck he gives me. His breathing is ragged in my ear, his grip rough and merciless, but I love it.

I love everything this man could give to me.

"That's my good girl," Sebastian groans, grinding up into me. "Fuck, you were made to clench this cock. Do it, baby," he orders. "Squeeze it tight for Daddy."

I mewl in pleasure, desperately clenching my inner walls around his cock. Sebastian swears, grunting in the dark of the alleyway as he thrusts into me, not caring who could hear us.

Not minding who could see.

The thought is like silver in my veins, and damn, he knows it. "Look at my sparrow, fucking with her skirt up around her waist for anyone to watch," he groans, reaching around to rub at my clit, making me shake and tremor. "This is what you need, isn't it, baby? Rough and dirty, like my good little whore."

His words drive me wild. His wicked fingers send me cresting. And his cock... Fuck, the thick, sweet drive of it sends me plummeting into ecstasy, my climax ripping through me with an explosion of pleasure.

I scream his name in the dark, over and over, as Sebastian grips my hair tighter, arches my body to his will, and fucks me through my orgasm and into the next.

"That's my good girl," he growls, pounding into me with an

animal fury. "Come all over Daddy's cock, get me nice and wet. And I'll return the favor. *Fuck...*"

He suddenly pulls out, and drags me around to face him, shoving me to my knees on the ground.

"Eyes on me," he demands, fisting himself furiously. "Don't you dare look away."

I couldn't if I tried. I stay there obediently on my knees below him, watching his climax take hold. He comes apart above me with a howl, painting my face and chest in thick ribbons of come as he shudders his release in the dark of the alleyway.

When it's over, he cups my cheek with his hand, panting. His eyes glow with dark triumph as he pushes some of the come into my mouth. "Look at you, baby. Fuck. All messed up."

I suck his thumb greedily, and he groans again. "I've got to get you home," he says, dragging me to my feet and pulling my dress down again. "The things I want to do to you... They'll arrest me for sure if we keep it up here."

"I don't know..." I manage, in heaven. "Want to bet?"

Sebastian chuckles, and tenderly wipes my face off before zipping up his pants and leading me out of the alleyway. My underwear is gone, the tattered remains left behind on the ground somewhere. I feel giddy, unable to remember the last time I felt so content.

The things this man can do to me...

We hurry back to the apartment, eager to pick up where we left off. But when we arrive back, there's a package waiting outside the door.

Sebastian lets us in, then opens it.

"It's my papers," he says, pulling out a passport first. He shows me the name listed on the fake document. "You're now looking at Steven Davies. Plain old Steve."

"You know, you do look like a Steve," I'm teasing, but my

happiness fades as I wonder what happens next. Is he going to disappear now? What does that mean for us?

"I'm not going anywhere without you," he says as if he's reading my mind. "Whatever happens next... It's up to the both of us to decide."

"Well, what do you want to happen?" I ask, looking to him carefully.

He looks back at me. "We could go anywhere. Do anything. Those plans we made at the cabin," he says, with a fond smile. "There's nothing to stop us following through now."

"You mean, a yacht in the Caribbean?"

"I'll bring the sunscreen," he quips, but I can't joke so easily, not with the stakes so high. We may have been able to pretend like nothing else matters for the last twenty-four hours, but there's still a killer out there. Richard. And Sebastian's name in ruins, paying for his uncle's crimes.

I think for a long moment.

"We can't just run." I finally say. "We can't let the world think you're a monster."

Sebastian gives a shrug. "I don't care."

I give him a look.

"I mean it," he says, drawing me closer, into his arms. "All that matters now is what you think of me. The two of us know the truth. Maybe that's enough."

I pause, thinking it over. I'm touched by his faith in me, and how willing he is to walk away from everything he's built. But even if he's willing to sacrifice everything...

I'm not.

"No," I finally answer, pulling back. "You know, ever since we met, I've been learning how complicated things can be. There's no such thing as black and white, most of the time. People make mistakes, and sometimes death is a senseless tragedy," I continue. "But this? Your father, Bianca's dad... The plane crash? No. This was murder, and Richard has gotten away with it for too long." My resolve grows. "That man left you to feel like a killer every day of your life. He came after us, after *me*," I add grimly. "I won't just walk away and let him win. He deserves justice, and we need to make him pay."

There's silence for a moment, and I can see Sebastian thinking it over. Then he gives a grim nod.

"You're right," he says quietly. "But this is my fight, I won't let you—"

"Tough," I cut him off, before he can try and pull something noble and self-sacrificing again. "And it became my fight the minute the bastard tried to blow me to pieces at twenty-thousand feet. In case you hadn't noticed, I'm not exactly the type to forgive and forget," I add with a dark smile.

Sebastian chuckles. "Oh, I've learned that the hard way."

"And Richard's about to learn it, too." I say. "So, we're agreed? No running. Not before we fight."

Sebastian takes my hand, then nods. "Time to make him pay," he agrees, pulling me into a hot, searing kiss.

I kiss him back, determination like steel in my veins. Richard better run, because between the two of us?

We know a thing or two about vengeance.

## Chapter 17

### *Avery*

It's tough to travel under the radar, but we don't have much of a choice. We might both have top-of-the-line fake IDs now, but Sebastian is still an easily recognizable man who's wanted by the police across the globe. Not only that, but if we're going to find a way to expose Richard, we need the element of surprise.

We decide to avoid airports and all the security the goes along with them. Instead, we travel overland by train from Venice, up through Switzerland and France. It takes a couple of days, hiding out in our first-class sleeper carriage, and making good use of the alone time—even if the narrow bunk barely holds Sebastian's weight, let alone the two of us.

We finally arrive in England in the afternoon, dressed in plain clothes and wearing both hats and sunglasses as we disembark the Eurostar train. "According to the gossip columns, Richard and your mom are planning a big anniversary party this weekend," I remark, trying to distract myself with the latest news, as we make our way to passport control.

"Uh huh?" Sebastian replies, looking more tense as the line inches forward.

"Kind of tasteless, if you ask me," I have to add, looking at the grainy newsprint photo of the couple, leaving some restaurant. "They haven't even found your body, and they're throwing a big soiree?"

"That's Richard," Sebastian says, scowling. "Probably thinks it's some kind of twisted celebration."

I wince, falling silent as we reach passport control. My nerves are tangled tightly, but the bored looking man barely glances twice at us, and we make it through without a hitch. But the border agents aren't the only people I'm worried about. The station concourse is crowded, and it should be easy to blend in, but that also means there are more eyes that could recognize Sebastian. There's also always a police presence in places like this, and I brace myself for a cry of recognition, or someone glancing our way too long.

We're trying to get out of here as fast as we can, so I'm keeping my head down and following along behind Seb as he leads me across the busy station concourse toward the exit. When he stops suddenly, I nearly run into him.

"What's wrong?" I ask frantically as he whips around to face me looking like he's seen a ghost.

"Old friends of my mother's, standing at the ticket counter. I don't think they saw me though."

He's ducking down as he explains, his eyes darting around until he grabs my arm and pulls me to a side hallway that leads to the restrooms.

"Well, I guess we're safe here unless one of them has to take a piss," I joke, trying to ignore my own panic. I can't believe our bad luck.

Sebastian says nothing, keeping his attention laser-focused in the direction of the ticket counter. He can't see it from here, but I know when the couple he's watching for walk by because he freezes with a deep frown on his face.

But a minute later, he lets out a long exhale. "Okay, I think the coast is clear."

I follow him out of the hallway, and we return to the main concourse. But we've barely made it three steps when I feel a hand on my shoulder.

"Excuse me," an unfamiliar voice says. My stomach drops, and I think about making a run for it, before forcing myself to turn with an innocent smile.

"Yes?"

It's a middle-aged woman, with a bland smile on her face. She's holding something out to me. "I think you dropped this."

What?

I'm still frozen, so Sebastian takes it from her. It's a scarf, one I bought back in Italy. "Thank you," he says smoothly. "You're very kind."

"Thanks!" I manage to blurt, before she smiles, and continues on her way.

I sigh with relief. "Let's just get out of here," I mumble, gripping Sebastian's hand tightly.

"Agreed."

We find the exit, and step outside, to the busy street beyond. There are taxis, busses, and a scrum of people here, too, but Sebastian leads me a couple of blocks away from the station, to a quiet side street where I can finally relax.

"That deserted island is looking pretty good about now," I comment, trying to shake off the tension.

"Having second thoughts?" Sebastian checks.

I shake my head. "No. And I've been thinking," I add. "We need to get the forensics guy on our side. He said he wouldn't testify about what he found, but without him, we have zero proof. He didn't keep a copy of the accident report, so it's just our word that the brakes were cut."

Sebastian nods. "I know. Perhaps if I talked to him myself, I could convince him to come forward and tell the truth. Either that, or I cut a large enough check that it would make up for the attention," he adds.

"You really think a payoff would work?" I ask, surprised.

"It did for Richard," he points out. "But either way, it's worth trying."

I agree, so we find a car rental service, and book a vehicle. It's not far to Brian's place, but we can't have anyone tracking our location, and it helps to spend the drive alone, away from prying eyes. I think about calling ahead and telling him we're on our way to see him, but I decide against it. The last thing we want is him panicking and refusing to even talk.

I glance over and see Sebastian frowning as he drives. "Everything OK?" I ask gently.

He sighs. "I'm just trying to put everything together in my mind. All this time. I believed the worst about myself, that it was all my fault," he says softly. "I killed my father, I hurt Scarlett... It's haunted me every minute of every day for over fifteen years. And now, it's hard to wrap my head around the truth. It wasn't my fault."

I put a supportive hand on his arm. "No, it wasn't."

"But Richard let me believe it was." Sebastian's jaw tightens. "I knew he was jealous of my dad for building Wolfe Capital into an empire, but I never would have believed he could do that to his own brother. The idea that jealousy would drive him to murder..."

I nod, chilled. "It's awful."

"It makes me sick to think about it." Sebastian's tone turns steely. "And he didn't even stop there. Richard stole my father's whole life. His company. His *wife*. What kind of man does that?"

I ache for the pain he must be going through.

"He won't get away with it," I vow. "We'll find a way to expose him. If Brian won't come forward with the truth, then we'll find someone else involved in the cover-up. Someone must have evidence."

Sebastian nods, as he pulls over outside Brian's house. There's only one car in the driveway, and as we approach the house, I can't hear the sound of the children like before.

"Hopefully, the kids are still in school, so that we can have time alone to talk." I say, as I ring the doorbell. Despite his pledge not to help any further, I feel hopeful we can talk him around. Surely between the two of us, we can find a way to convince him to help us expose Richard.

But there's no answer at the door. Sebastian rings it again, but still... No answer. No other signs of life, except the lights are on inside, and I can hear music too, maybe from the radio.

"What do you think?" Sebastian asks.

I look around. "I think he could be avoiding us," I say. "Let's go check."

I lead him around the side of the house, looking in the windows as we go. It looks like someone's home, judging from the view into the kitchen: There's a lunch plate on the table, with a half-eaten sandwich, and the kettle is whistling on the stove, with documents spread nearby, as if—

Wait a minute.

"That's weird," I remark, feeling like something is wrong.

"What is?" Sebastian asks.

"The tea kettle. You wouldn't just leave it boiling like that. Not when it's making such a noise."

We pause, waiting, listening to the high-pitched whistle.

Nobody comes.

Sebastian circles to the back door. "It's open," he says grimly. Sure enough, it's ajar.

We exchange a worried look. Sebastian pulls his sleeve down to cover his hand and pushes it wider. "Hello?" he calls.

"Brian?" I follow him into the kitchen. "Brian, it's me, Avery."

Silence. It's eerily quiet, and I feel unease creep down my spine. But I continue forward, heading for the office. I remember it's just down this hallway, with the door—

"Avery, don't!"

Sebastian calls from behind me, but it's too late. I've already pushed the door wider and stepped into the room.

I scream.

Brian is slumped over his desk, a gun clutched in one hand, blood pooling on the papers there from a gaping bullet wound in his temple.

He's dead.

# Chapter 18

## *Avery*

"Oh my god!" Panic grips me, propelling me forward towards his body.

"Avery, no!" Sebastian pulls me back.

"But we have to help him!" I cry, frantically looking around.

"It's too late," Sebastian holds me firmly, turning me so I'm facing him. "Avery, it's over. He's gone."

I gasp for air. "No..."

"We have to go," he says, his voice urgent in my ear. "Come on, Avery. We need to get the fuck out of here, *now*."

I'm too shocked to resist as Sebastian drags me out of the room, back through the kitchen and out of the open door.

"But they'll find him like that," I blurt, horrified. "His family... The kids... Sebastian—"

"Go."

He hustles me back to the car, and practically shoves me into the passenger seat. Then he drives off, cursing under his breath as we follow the road away from his house, and out into the open countryside. I sit there, reeling, in shock from what

I've just seen, until Sebastian finally pulls off the main road, and down a winding country lane, finally coming to a stop beside an old fence in the middle of nowhere, with nothing but trees and fields for miles around.

My sob shatters the silence. I crumple into tears as the shock finally leaves my body. Sebastian pulls me closer, into a tight hug. "It's okay," he tells me, reassuring "It's going to be okay."

It comes back to me in flashes, the dark red pooling on his desk. "But I... I don't understand it," I sniff. "Why would he do something like that?"

"He didn't."

I raise my head to look into his grim face. "What?" I ask, shocked.

"Brian didn't kill himself," Sebastian says bluntly. "The back door wasn't just open. It was forced. With a crowbar would be my guess. By whoever staged that suicide scene. You're right," he adds, "A man who'd do anything to protect his family would never put them through that kind of grief, finding him like that."

"Oh my god," I whisper, stunned by the violence of the scene. Then I realize, "We must have just missed them! The kettle, it was still boiling. If Brian had put it on the stove, then he couldn't have been dead long."

Sebastian nods. "Maybe..."

"If we'd just been faster," I say with a guilty pang. "God, if I hadn't stopped to buy that snack—"

"Don't say that," Sebastian cuts me off. "If we'd been there any sooner, we would be dead, too. It's Richard's handiwork," he adds, with fury in his eyes. "He's tying up loose ends."

I shiver. "Who else would he go after?" I wonder.

"I don't know." Sebastian frowns. "Anyone connected to the crash, any possible witnesses..."

I gasp with a sudden realization. "Oh my God, Seb. What about Scarlett?"

All the color drains from his face. "Fuck!"

He snatches up one of the burner phones we bought, and quickly dials. "Scarlett?" he tries, before cursing. "It's her voicemail."

"Try again. I'll drive," I add. We trade seats, and I quickly get back on the road again, driving fast towards the main motorway, as Sebastian places call after call. He keeps getting voicemail, his alarm clear in every word.

"It's me, I can't explain, but you have to get out of the house," he says, gripping the phone so tightly his knuckles are white. "Go to the village, stay somewhere with people around. I'm on my way to get you. Please, be careful!"

I drive faster. Sebastian hangs up, and directs me down the winding country roads, our anxiety growing. We're an hour away, and there's no shortcuts to be taken. All I can do is pray that I'm wrong about Richard. That he wouldn't hurt an innocent, not like this.

"Up there," Sebastian barks, pointing to the driveway. He flings the door open and scrambles out before I've even brought the car to a stop. I hit the brakes, and quickly follow him as he races inside.

"Scarlett!"

I hear an agonized yell, and my heart stops. I hurry down the hallway and find Sebastian on his knees in the living room.

He's cradling his sister's lifeless body in his arms.

"Wake up," he's yelling, desperately shaking her limp frame. "Scarlett, you have to wake up!"

I look wildly around. There's an empty pill bottle on the floor beside her. It's an overdose—or something made to look like one.

"Get her to the car," I order Sebastian, springing into

action. "We don't have time to wait for an ambulance. We have to get her to an ER, now!"

He stares at me blankly, already numb. "Sebastian," I rush closer, and feel Scarlett's throat for a pulse.

There.

"She's still breathing," I tell him. "It's not too late. Come on!"

The drive to the hospital is a blur, breaking the speed limit on the narrow country roads. Sebastian rushes Scarlett inside, and soon she's swept up to an operating room, and we're left to pace the waiting room in agonized silence for hours. Waiting for news.

"I'll kill him," Sebastian vows, fists clenched at his sides. "I'll goddamn tear him apart."

"Later," I say softly. I'm not about to argue with him now. His sister means the world to him; he's spent his life trying to protect her. I can only imagine the helpless rage he feels right now. "Let's just keep it together now. For Scarlett."

I see a familiar looking doctor emerge, and rush over to greet him. "What happened?" I demand frantically. "Is she OK?"

"She'll live."

I sag with relief. "Oh, thank God."

"We pumped her stomach," he continues, looking grave. "But she was very lucky. If you hadn't found her when you did..."

If Richard hadn't tried to kill her.

"I need to see her," Sebastian says. It's not a request, but the doctor hesitates anyway.

"Please," I add. "Just for a moment? We're her friends," I add, lying.

He looks at me sympathetically. "Make it quick. She needs to rest. And don't upset her."

I can't imagine her becoming any more upset than she must already be, but I nod. We head upstairs and find her in a private room at the end of the hall. Scarlett is lying in bed, looking pale and weak, but her eyes widen with shock at the sight of us.

"Sebastian?" She looks back and forth between us. "H-how are you here? Am I dead too?"

"No," he says gently, moving closer the sit by the bed and take her hand. "I'm alive. We both are. It's a long story,' he adds, and she lets out a sleepy sigh, relaxing.

"Good. I've missed you, big brother."

"I've missed you too," Sebastian looks grim. "What happened to you? Who did this?"

He sounds so calm, but I know there's a storm brewing inside of him.

Scarlett's forehead scrunches as she thinks. "I don't know... I was in the paddock. Then... I heard something behind me, but before I could turn around, there was pain in the back of my head. And... I-I woke up here. I didn't take the pills," she adds, tearful. "I know they're saying I overdosed, but didn't relapse, I promise."

Her voice cracks, and Sebastian leans over to hug her, whispering soothing words in her ear.

"I know, sweetheart. It's OK. It's all going to be OK."

I tactfully move away, to the window, leaving them to their murmured conversation. Then I see movement down below on the sidewalk. A black car pulls up, and two familiar figures climb out, hurrying to the main entrance.

Richard and Trudy.

*Shit.*

"We have to go," I say, moving back to grab Sebastian.

"What?"

"Unwelcome visitors," I tell him meaningfully. "Family."

Rage flashes in Sebastian's eyes.

"Scarlett, you can't tell anyone we were here, OK?" I tell her gently, pulling Sebastian away. "It's a secret. Not even your mum."

She looks to Sebastian, and he nods. "I'll send someone to protect you," he vows. "Just get better, I'll see you soon."

We slip out of the room just in time. At the far end of the hall, the elevator doors open, and I bundle Sebastian into an empty room before anyone can spot us.

We can hear Richard talking as they get closer, comforting Trudy with fake concern in his voice. "It must be the stress from her brother's death. We can try rehab again. I'm sure it'll be OK."

Seb's fists clench with fury. "I should just go kill him right now and be done with it."

"Not here," I tell him, blocking the door. "Think, Sebastian, if you just attack him out of nowhere, then his story still stands. You'll be called a killer, and he'll get away with all his crimes. We have to fix this, the right way."

"But how?" Sebastian demands. I can see the pain in his eyes, and the raw anger haunting every word. "He's come after you, he hurt my sister... When will it be time to make him pay?"

"Soon," I promise him, with all my heart. "Soon, this will all be over."

## Chapter 19

## *Sebastian*

I thought I knew what fury was. I'm a man of control, but that doesn't mean I haven't been driven to the edge before, by business rivals and traitorous friends. By Avery, more than once, when I discovered all her lies.

But nothing compares to the cold, hard rage that burns inside me, knowing what Richard has done.

After Avery practically drags me from the hospital, I make a call and summon the best security around, a former Navy SEAL who comes highly recommended. He won't leave Scarlett's side, and if anyone asks, she'll say he's her new boyfriend. That should keep Richard and his heavies at bay, at least for a little while.

Knowing she's protected, even without me, we finally head back to London, and a discreet townhouse that Saint owns. Avery says we need time to regroup and figure the best way to tackle the Richard issue. If she's hoping I'll take a beat and calm down, she's wrong. Every passing minute just fuels my anger, knowing that man is walking the earth.

Preying on my family. Coming after the people I love the most.

It has to end. *Now*.

"The man is smart," Avery says grimly, as we review everything we know. "Destroying the evidence, getting rid of any potential witnesses... There's no proof left, of anything."

"He's created the perfect narrative," I agree bitterly, pacing in the narrow living room, restless. Saint's townhouse is the height of luxury, but I still feel caged here. "Everyone thinks I'm the bad guy here, and that he's the only trustworthy one in the room."

"Yeah... About that," Avery gives a wince. "Sorry."

I exhale. "It's not your fault," I tell her sincerely. "Exposing that I was the one behind the wheel for the accident... You thought you were doing the right thing."

"And Richard got to me, too," she says with a scowl. "I never liked the guy, but I didn't think he was capable of murder."

She pauses. "Maybe we're going at this the wrong way," she says, looking thoughtful. "Maybe it isn't proof we really need."

"You're right," I say grimly. "Maybe this is a problem I need to solve for myself."

"No!" Avery protests immediately.

"You can't tell me you care if he lives or dies?" I demand, and she gives me a look.

"Not him, you." Avery glares. "And if there's one thing I've learned from the past few months, it's that no vengeance ever works out the way you plan. If you go after Richard, you could wind up hurt. Arrested. Or even worse: Dead."

I shake my head. "I wouldn't be so stupid."

"And I won't give you the choice," Avery says fiercely. "I've just found you, and I refuse to let you go again. So if you try anything... Well, I'll just kill you myself."

I would never have thought a promise of murder would warm my heart, but seeing Avery's devotion helps ease the anger burning in my chest.

For the first time, I'm not alone. She has my back. And I need to protect her too, no matter what.

I realize Avery has fallen silent, looking thoughtful. I know that expression well: She's planning something.

"What is it?"

"Our whole problem here is that it's his word against ours, right?" she says slowly. "He's the one with the big deal profile as the new CEO of Wolfe Capital. Even bigger now that everyone thinks you're dead," she points out. "He's been playing it up, courting the press, because he loves the status. I mean, this whole big anniversary party he's hosting with your mom this weekend, that's just a big excuse for attention. So why don't we use that against him? Use his own words to expose him."

"You mean, set him up to confess somehow?" I ask, frowning. "He would never fall for it."

"Wouldn't he?" Avery smiles, her eyes bright now. "The man has an ego the size of London—plus, I bet he's just dying to crow about his brilliant plans. He thinks we're dead, remember? That he's gotten away with it all. If we show up and somehow shock him into a confession..."

"He couldn't help himself," I finish, feeling optimistic for the first time in days. "He always wants to be the smartest guy in the room." I pause. "But still, it's a big risk. He might not play ball."

"We'll make him," she says, steely. "There's no other choice."

. . .

We go over our plan for the rest of the night, thinking through every angle. Avery is in her element, determined to see this through. The thought is strangely comforting. I'd bet on her, any day. Avery has proven, she can be brilliant and ruthless, stopping at nothing to get her revenge.

I can admire that heartless streak in her, now it's not directed at me.

"We should take a break," Avery says, pushing our scribbled papers aside. She gets up, stretching with a yawn. "Do you want something to eat?"

I shake my head.

"We could put on a movie, watch some TV..." she suggests.

"No. I can't think about anything right now except this."

"Are you sure about that?"

When I look up, Avery has a playful smile on her lips. "It seems to me like you need to relax," she continues, strolling over to me. She places her hands on my chest, pressing closer, but I shake my head, still distracted.

"Not now."

I pull away, my mind too preoccupied with everything going on to even consider relaxation. But Avery isn't so easily dissuaded.

"That sounds an awful lot like a challenge," she says, gently pushing me back so I sit back on the couch.

Slowly, she straddles my lap.

My pulse kicks. Even with everything, my body can't help but respond to her. She presses closer, her breasts brushing my chest as she grinds a little on my lap, still playful and teasing. "See, you're so tense... There's nothing else we can do tonight."

She trails her hands over me, locking her hands behind my neck as she leans in for a kiss. Damn. Her mouth is soft and hot, and I feel a familiar desire ignite inside of me. My cock grows hard as she writhes against it, teasing me.

Her lips trail along my jaw, and she whispers in my ear, "Tell me what to do. I need another lesson."

*Fuck.*

She knows just what to say to captivate me, and to send every other thought racing from my mind.

"You need it, baby?" I say, my voice thick.

She nods, holding eye contact as she bounces on my cock. "I want to learn. Something new. Something naughty. Teach me…"

And damn, there's no going back now. Now when she's so soft and sweet in my arms, begging for instruction.

Not when I need a release that only she can provide. A chance to forget about everything else, just for a moment.

A way to feel like I'm still in control.

I take her wrists and pin them behind her, holding her back so I can look her in the eye. "Then get on your knees, baby. Unbuckle my belt, and open wide."

Her eyes flare with passion, and she scrambles off my lap, eager to do what I say. I sit back into the sofa, already feeling that surge of power take me over as I watch her nimble fingers open my buckle and unbutton my pants. She lowers to her knees, lips already wet with anticipation as she palms my thick cock in her hands.

I sigh in satisfaction.

"Swallow it, Sparrow," I growl, loving the flush that spreads over her delicate skin at my orders. "Open wide for Daddy and take every last inch."

She moans as she dips her head and eagerly parts her lips to suck me into her warm, wet mouth. *Fuck.* She feels incredible, and looks just as hot, eyes raised to me obediently, eager to please.

"Like that," I groan in appreciation. "Just like that, baby. Don't stop."

She starts to work me, licking my thick shaft and swirling her tongue over the head.

I pull her hair back out of her face so that I can watch her as she bobs up and down, taking me deeper until the blunt head of my cock hits the back of her throat.

She gags, but I don't stop, gently thrusting further, not breaking pace. "You can do it, baby," I mutter encouragement, fisting her silken hair in my hands. "Breathe through it, don't stop."

She moans in answer, sucking me deeper, so goddamn eager to please. Avery is magnificent and strong-willed, and sexy as hell when she's ready to burn everything down, but when she gives me the privilege of her surrender like this...

There's nothing like it in the world.

Her hot mouth is getting me close—too close—so I drag her up and lay her out on the couch beneath me. She gazes up at me, breathless, looking like a work of art. The way her lips part, and her cheeks flush. The slight arch of her back. The glistening wetness between her legs...

She's a goddess.

I strip off my clothes, consumed now with the powerful urge to take her. Claim her. Sink into her sweetness until she's crying my name.

"Seb..." she whispers.

"Too quiet, baby," I growl, roughly taking her legs, and spreading them wider. Baring her glistening cunt to me. "Scream it for me."

Her eyes widen in excitement, and then I'm thrusting inside her in one brutal stroke. Driving deep.

*Coming home.*

Avery's voice echoes with a pleasured cry, and she arches up, pulling me closer taking me even deeper into her tight, wet heat.

*Goddamn.*

I roar at the feel of her, clenching me like a fucking vise. "Fuck, baby..." I groan, thrusting into her again. "You feel so fucking good."

"Yes," she moans, writhing against me. "Sebastian... Please."

"How does my baby want it?" I croon, grinding up inside her, just how she likes. Avery whimpers, flushed and bright-eyed beneath me. "You want to fuck like my good girl... or my sweet little whore?"

"Anything..." she gasps, clinging onto me. "Anything you want. Just don't *stop*..."

Her voice breaks as I fuck into her again, but even though all I want is to screw her into oblivion, I keep control, slowing my pace.

She wanted a lesson. And fuck, I'm going to give it to her.

With superhuman restraint, I pull out, and flip her onto her hands and knees. "Ass up, baby," I demand, landing a stinging slap on one lush cheek.

Avery yelps at the impact, but when she glances back at me, I can see the fever bright in her eyes. She wriggles her ass, as if asking for more.

Goddamn.

I spank her harshly, then grip a handful of her hair, and thrust into her wet cunt from behind, sending her body slamming forward into the arm of the sofa with the impact.

"Yes!" she screams, grinding back against my cock.

Fuck, she feels incredible from this angle, and I pound into her like an animal, riding her relentlessly.

Her whimpers turn into pleading mewls, "Sebastian... Please! Oh. Oh..." Avery writhes, her breasts bouncing. Her pussy clenches desperately around me, and I know she's close.

I know what she needs to go over the edge.

Running my hands over her body, I squeeze one breast, tweaking at her nipple, before trailing my hand lower, to pet and toy with her swollen clit. She moans louder, thrusting back and forth between my hand and cock, chasing the friction. "I'm close," she gasps, tensing. "Oh fuck, Seb—"

"Not yet."

I land a light slap between her legs, then withdraw my hand. Avery sobs in protest. "You wanted a lesson, didn't you, sweetheart?"

I slow my thrusts, even as my cock screams for more. Then, deliberately, I part her round ass cheeks, and spit.

Avery's breath hitches as my saliva coats her tight, forbidden bud.

"Sebastian?" Her movements falter, but I keep thrusting into her pussy in slow, measured strokes.

"You belong to me now," I growl, feeling a wave of pierce possession. "Every part of you, baby. Even *here*."

Avery gasps, as I nudge my index finger against her asshole. "Seb..." she blurts, and I can hear the hesitation in her voice. "I've never..."

"I know."

Fuck, I can't stop the surge of power that crashes through me, knowing all over again that I'll be the first to teach her.

The only one.

"Just relax," I order her, rubbing softly. I sink my cock into her pussy again, as my finger nudges and explores, making her whole body tremble. "You want to be my good girl, don't you?" I croon, knowing how she responds to those simple words.

Avery moans, her body relaxing a little. "Yes, please..."

"So take it," I order darkly, nudging my finger inside her tight channel. I already feel my own climax build. Fuck, coiling in the base of my spine, a tidal wave waiting to be unleashed. "Take what I give you, baby. This body... It belongs to me."

"Seb..." Avery shudders, taking my finger deeper, and damn, all I can think it how tight she's going to be, opening for my cock.

She moans, getting used to the sensation, as I pick up my pace again. Fuck, I can't hold back long now, and as Avery's body begins to move with me, *welcoming me,* I feel my climax coil.

"Is this what you want?" I demand, fucking her deeper. Invading her cunt and her ass, so tight for me. All mine.

"Yes," she cries, gasping. Begging for me. "Don't stop! Oh god, don't stop..."

I feel the dark pleasure rising, out of control. Oh *fuck.* "Come for me, Sparrow," I growl, grinding my cock deep, as she clenches around me, her cries of pleasure echoing. "Come on, baby. Milk me all the way."

"Seb!" she screams out, her pussy going off in spasms, her whole body shaking as I come into her with a roar. The pleasure surges, blotting out the world, so there's nothing but the two of us, Avery so tight around me, taking everything I give her, still moaning and begging for more.

My girl. My *world.*

And whatever plans we've made, I know I'd rather die before I let anyone hurt her again.

## Chapter 20

## *Avery*

There's no time to waste. Sebastian's security guy may be guarding Scarlett around the clock, but we have no way of knowing if Richard is still planning to silence her for good. Or who else he's got on his list of loose ends.

This has to end.

Tonight.

I fix my makeup in the bathroom mirror, my heart already racing with nerves and anticipation. It's the night of Richard and Trudy's big anniversary party, and we've decided it's the perfect stage for our plan. Hundreds of people will be gathering at their country estate, with media and VIPs schmoozing everywhere. Richard will be on top of the world.

And it'll be my job to bring him back down to earth again.

"You look stunning."

Sebastian's voice makes me turn. "You think so?" I smile and strike a nervous pose. I'm wearing a gorgeous one-shoulder dress the color of champagne. It fits like a second skin, showing off my figure in a way that leaves nothing to the imagination. I have simple diamonds in my ears and hanging around my neck. I look elegant. Regal.

Like a queen.

"It was very thoughtful of them to make it a masquerade party," I add, brandishing my elaborate Mardi Gras mask, covered with plumes of golden feathers to match the dress. "At least we know I'll be able to sneak in, incognito."

Sebastian nods, but he still looks tense, moving closer to adjust my strap. "I don't like this part of the plan. I don't want you anywhere near Richard."

"I know, but it's necessary," I reassure him, smoothing my palms over the lapels of his tuxedo. "Besides, people always underestimate me. You did," I tease. "Remember when you thought I was just an innocent sweetheart?"

He chuckles. "I learned soon enough, you're a force to be reckoned with."

"And soon, Richard is going to find out, too."

We drive through the dark to the country, then pull off a side road before we reach the estate. Sebastian steers along the dark track through the trees, then parks in a hidden spot just beyond the perimeter. From here, we can see the house is lit up, music and laughter echoing into the darkness, as a trail of cars arrives down the driveway, and people in cocktail attire greet each other and enter the house.

"Ready?" Sebastian asks me, looking tense. I know, he doesn't want to leave my side, but this plan will only work if I go in there alone. He's way too conspicuous to blend into the crowd for long, and even with a mask, there'll be no mistaking his dominating frame.

I take a deep breath, and nod. For all our plans and hypotheticals back in London, it's only hitting me now just how high the stakes are.

I'm about to stroll into a house with the man who wants me dead. Who's left a trail of dead bodies behind him in his quest for wealth and power—and who won't hesitate to kill again, if I try to stand in his way.

"You don't have to do this," Sebastian says, as if reading my thoughts. He takes my face between his hands, cradling it as he gazes into my eyes. "I told you, we can run. Find that yacht and leave this all behind."

I feel an ache of longing, but I know, it's not real. "But what about Scarlett?" I remind him. "Your mom… Bianca, and Brian's family… It would be selfish of us to disappear into the sunset, when they deserve justice, too."

Sebastian nods, his jaw set. His eyes already steely with determination. "I know," he says. "But you don't have to do this—"

"Yes, I do." I give him a kiss, my heart aching, but full. "It's you and me, together. No matter what."

Seb kisses my forehead, then releases me. "You have everything you need?"

I nod, patting my bag. We stopped by a tech store and picked up some goodies before making the trip. I have a panic button that's connected to a receiver that Sebastian has, just in case, plus some other things. "See you soon," he promises, then sets off towards the woods to the side of the house. His shadow is quickly swallowed in the darkness.

I gulp. It's up to me now.

I make my way across the meadow, and down towards the house, out of sight. No one notices me slip through the gardens, and I circle around to near where the line of cars is backing up the driveway; drivers leaning on their horns in protest as the caravan slowly snakes closer to the main doors.

"Get a move on!" a posh sounding voice echoes from one of the limousines, and laughter follows.

"This is taking forever!"

"It's not far. Come on, it'll be quicker to walk!"

A group of half-a-dozen people emerges from the limo, all dressed to the nines, clutching evening bags and tuxedo jackets, shrieking with tipsy laughter.

Clearly, the party started early for them.

"But my heels…" one of the women protests, waving her mask around.

"I'll carry you. Hop on!" There's more laughter as she clambers onto one of the men in a drunken piggyback, and they all make their way up the gravel driveway towards the house.

I step out of the shadows and join them as they approach the security guards on duty, acting like I'm a part of their group.

"Isn't this a hoot?" the girl riding on his back cries to me, and I give a big smile.

"Such a riot!" I agree, making my voice plummy, like theirs.

"I just love your dress," another tells me, beaming.

"Thanks!" I smile back. "Although, I wish I'd worn flat shoes. Nobody told me it would be a hike!"

"I know!"

The girls chorus in agreement as we bustle up to the doors. My pulse kicks as one of the guys produces a fistful of printed invitations, and waves them at a bouncer, who tries to examine them as the group pushes inside, still laughing and chatting at full volume.

"Miss?" one of the security guards tries to stop me, but I just gesture vaguely at the others.

"I'm with them!" I call, and let the group sweep me inside, as the guard turns, distracted by another new arrival.

I catch my breath, delighted.

I'm in!

I slip away from my new friends and take a beat to look around and absorb the scene. The last time Sebastian and I were here, it was for a casual family dinner. Tonight, there's nothing casual about the scene. Richard and Trudy have gone all out with the opulent masquerade theme. There are gold and silver flower arrangements everywhere, a huge live jazz band at one end of the great room, and dancing spilling out onto the terrace beyond. In one room, a lavish buffet is groaning with fine foods: massive, tiered seafood towers of oysters and lobster, caviar boats, and in the next, bartenders craft fancy cocktails and pour champagne.

I shoot a glance at the glass mezzanine level above the main party. Richard's office is up there, and I'm dying to take a look, but I have to stick to the plan. The crowd is huge, and having a great time, dancing, chatting, and even gambling in a room staged to look like an exclusive casino, with card dealers in matching uniforms. And holding court over the whole party, beaming happily, is Sebastian's mother, Trudy. And by her side...

Richard.

I slip back behind a pillar, as they move closer through the crowd, greeting old friends, their conversation audible nearby.

"Thank you for coming," Richard glad-hands everyone, puffed up and beaming in his designer suit. "We thought it was high time we look to the future, after everything this family has gone through. You know, times of tragedy teach us to treasure the good times, and that's what we're celebrating here tonight."

Psychotic asshole, throwing a party after everything he's done.

My blood boils, and I'm tempted to go confront him now, but I force myself to slip away, and take deep breaths to calm down. *Stick to the plan,* I remind myself.

Soon enough, they'll know the truth about him.

I slip down a back hallway, remembering Sebastian's instructions. He drew me a layout of the house, and I recall it now, heading away from the party, and down a corridor towards the kitchens. He told me there was a side door, leading to the outside from a utility room, and I check every door that I pass, searching for the right one.

"Excuse me?"

A voice makes me whirl around. "Yes?" I yelp, startled.

*Shit.*

It's one of the catering staff, with a tray of hors d'oeuvres in her arms. "This area is off-limits to the guests," she says politely. "Staff only."

"Really?" I try with wide-eyed innocence. "I'm so sorry, I was looking for the bathroom."

"Back that way," she points.

"I know," I wince, "Except they were all occupied, and that champagne goes right through me! Is there one here I could just nip into for a moment? Please?"

The woman relents. "There's one just down the hall," she points. "Don't tell anyone I let you, though."

"My lips are sealed!"

She turns to return to the party, and I wait until she's out of sight before finally locating the utility room.

*Yes!* I hurry past the laundry machines to the exterior door, and check that it's unlocked, then find a box of laundry powder to wedge it open.

There. Sebastian should be able to sneak in the back now, without anyone noticing.

I sent up a silent prayer that the rest of the evening goes just as smoothly, then return to the party. I mingle discreetly, on edge, one eye on the clock as I count down to ten p.m.. Every passing moment is torture, and my nerves are on edge.

Whatever promises Sebastian has made to me, I've seen the

raw fury in his eyes. There are only two ways tonight is ending. Either Richard is led off in handcuffs, exposed for all his crimes.

Or someone winds up dead.

Finally, the clock strikes, drowned out by the music and chatter of the party. But I hear every chime ring out.

It's time.

I look around for my target. Richard has just finished up chatting with a group of important looking older men. He heads back through the party, to the casino room, where he takes a seat at one of the tables, and gestures for champagne. His laughter echoes, smug, as I approach the room, and I have to fight to stay calm.

I should be used to smiling through my rage, but somehow, knowing this man has hurt the one person I care about now more than anything...

Sebastian isn't the only one with pure rage running in his veins.

Making sure my masquerade mask is fastened securely in place, I take a seat at the same game as Richard and smile pleasantly across the table. "Room for one more?" I coo lightly, and he gives me a smarmy grin, his gaze focused on my chest, not my face.

"The more the merrier. Let's play."

Game on.

## Chapter 21

### *Avery*

As the dealer begins to pass out our cards, the irony isn't lost on me. This whole mission started at the poker table, and now I'm right back here for the end.

"What do you say we make things interesting?" Richard chortles, checking out his cards. "I'm in for ten g's."

There's a titter of laughter, but everyone at the table agrees.

"Make that twenty," I say coolly, and he glances over, surprised.

"And you are...?" he frowns, clearly trying to place me.

I give a mysterious shrug. "Oh, nobody to you, I'm sure."

*Just the woman who's going to reveal your murderous past.*

The game gets underway, with players discarding cards, and sussing out their competition. The bets rise higher, but I couldn't care less about the cards I'm holding. I bluff fearlessly, like I have money to burn. There's only one person I'm watching.

Richard.

I'm playing a different kind of game, and no one at the table knows it. And in my game, I hold all the cards.

"You're quite the player," Richard remarks, as I raise his bet another twenty thousand pounds. I take a sip of my champagne and ignore the way my skin crawls when Richard's eyes dip down to my cleavage.

"You too," I say coolly. "You have a real 'take no prisoners' style. Or it should be... Leave no witnesses?" I add lightly. My tone is so breezy, none of the other players catch the remark, but Richard does. He pauses, frowning at me.

I smile back, hidden behind my mask.

"How do we know you, again?" he asks.

I shrug. "Oh, I'm more of a family friend. Although, we have several mutual friends. Brian Kendall, for example," I say lightly, naming the forensics expert who Richard had killed. "In fact, we were just talking, the other day. He had plenty to say about you."

Richard chokes on his drink, spluttering in shock.

*Bullseye.*

He looks across the table at me, and his expression changes. Recognition, and then confusion, dawning in his eyes.

He knows it's me. He just can't imagine *how*.

"Kendall, you say?" Richard says, recovering. "Poor man. Heard he died tragically. It's happening too often, these days."

"Isn't it just?" I narrow my eyes. "His family must be devastated."

"Of course." Richard holds my gaze, and I see the flash of nastiness he usually manages to hide. "If only he'd made different choices, perhaps things wouldn't have gone this way."

I control my temper. There's no point fighting here. Now that the hook is baited, it's time to reel him in.

"Whoops, I guess I fold." I set my cards down and rise to my feet. "It's been fun, but I think it's time I was moving on."

I give a little wave, and then sashay away, making sure that

I'm walking slow enough for Richard to see exactly where I'm heading.

Upstairs.

I catch my breath on the landing, my hands trembling with nerves. I might be cool and calm on the outside, but inside, my heart is pounding out of my chest.

Will it work? We're betting on Richard following me himself for answers, but he could just as easily call security, and have me dragged out.

I need to act fast.

I make my way down the hallway to Richard's office, with its flashy glass-walled mezzanine and views over the back terrace. There's a box of cigars on the desk, and a bag of golf clubs resting near the door: The gentleman's sanctuary, with photographs of Richard posing with politicians and celebrities. Taking the small video camera out of my purse, I set it up carefully between framed pictures on the bookcase, making sure it's at just the right level to record what happens in the room.

I hear footsteps in the hallway, and I suddenly wish that Sebastian could be here with me. He fought me on this so many times, but I was firm. The whole plan hinges on Richard incriminating himself, but there no way he'll do that if Sebastian is in the room.

So, it's all down to me.

The steps get louder, and I strengthen my resolve to do this. It's time to finally put an end to this.

The office door closes with a click. I turn around and meet Richard's calculating stare.

"Avery Carmichael..." he smirks. "Look who's risen from the dead."

## Chapter 22

### *Avery*

I watch as Richard closes the door behind us, and steps closer into the room.

"Surprise," I quip dryly. "Turns out, I wasn't quite ready to leave this mortal coil just yet. Despite your best efforts," I add. "Tell me, did you plant that bomb on the plane yourself, or hire some lackey to do it for you?"

Richard chuckles. "I don't know what you mean," he replies smugly. "I'm delighted to see you again. We all thought you'd perished in the crash."

"So you figured you'd celebrate with a twenty-piece band," I remark, gesturing to the party still raging below. "Real respectful."

"Haven't you heard? It's a celebration of life." Richard stalks closer. "So, I have to assume, if you're still alive, then my nephew was also lucky enough to cheat death?"

I smile. "Let me guess, you'd be delighted to see him too?"

"And concerned, of course, that he faces justice for his crimes."

"And which crimes are those?" I decide we've danced

around the truth long enough. "Cutting the brakes on your brother's car to try and kill him? No, wait, that was you."

Annoyance flashes on Richard's face. "So, you did talk to Kendall," he muses, almost to himself. "I did wonder how much he told you."

"Everything," I vow. "All about you covering up the forensics and paying him off to change his report and destroy the car."

"Then it's a pity he's no longer with us to back up your outlandish claims." Richard is still smug, thinking there's no evidence against him.

It's time to shake that belief.

"I don't need his testimony," I say calmly, bluffing just as hard as I did downstairs. "He gave me a copy of his original report."

Richard pauses. "You're lying. He burned it, the only one."

I inhale in a rush. Already, he's just incriminated himself without realizing. I need to push him further. Over the edge.

"That's just what he told you," I insist, "He kept a copy, as insurance. Protection, in case you came after him. He hated what he'd done. He wanted me to expose you."

"No." Richard shakes his head, but I see a vein bulging in his forehead.

"Yes. You know, a cold-blooded crime like that takes planning," I continue, "You didn't kill your brother in a rage, or the spur-of-the-moment. You plotted, waiting for your chance. You must have really hated him, huh?"

Richard doesn't reply.

"But of course you did. After all, he was everything you would never be," I continue. "Handsome, beloved, wealthy beyond your wildest dreams. That must have burned you up inside, huh? Watching his life soar, while you were stuck loitering in his shadows, a pale imitation of Patrick's success.

Tell me, what was it like for you, seeing your little brother surpass all your wildest dreams?"

"Shut up," he snaps, and I know I'm getting under his skin.

"You must have just been *sick* with jealousy. After all, he had everything and what did that leave you with? Nothing at all. No respect. No fame. No love."

My voice is taunting, and I can see his anger rising, but it's not enough. Not yet.

"Is that why you killed him?" I coo, moving closer. "You didn't just want to take him out of the picture, you wanted to *be* him. But the sad truth is, you're still trying. You couldn't live up to him when he was alive, what made you think you could do it once he was dead? Everyone still compares you to him, and you fall short." I add, mocking. "You always will. You're not as smart, not as driven. Even Trudy probably imagines Patrick when you're in bed together—"

SMACK.

Richard backhands me across the face, sending me stumbling with the force of the blow. "Shut up!" he yells, finally breaking. "Shut the fuck up!"

I press a palm to my stinging cheek. I taste blood, and my ears are ringing. But I can't stop now.

"Is that why you cut his brakes?" I demand, straightening up again. "So you could step into his shoes and live the life you thought you deserved? What's a little murder between brothers, I bet Patrick never even realized how much you loathed him. Never even noticed how you felt."

"That self-satisfied idiot never noticed a damn thing," Richard spits out, his voice ringing with rage. "He just sailed through life, like he was so much better than the rest of us. He never had to work for anything, it was all just handed to him on a silver platter. And meanwhile, I..." His fists clench at his sides. "I'm the one who deserved it! I was the one with the big ideas, even though Patrick got all the credit. He thought he was so fucking clever," he adds with a bitter laugh. "But he never saw it coming, did he?"

"The crash," I say, my heart pounding. "You cut the brakes on his car, and then covered it up, when Sebastian lost control of the vehicle."

Richard smiles dangerously, an unhinged glint in his eye. "It was easy. Hell, I should have done it years ago, been free of him sooner."

There it is. A confession. And even after everything, it still chills me to see him so unapologetic, reveling in his murder like it's some kind of victory.

"But the other driver, Sebastian and his sister... They were only kids," I find myself protesting. "Didn't you care about them?"

"Collateral damage," Richard shrugs. "Of course, it would have been better if they'd died too. Fewer heirs to squabble over the company. But Scarlett was in no shape to be a threat to me, especially not after her stay in Larkspur." A cruel grin twists his face. "And as for your dear Sebastian... As long as he thought the crash was his fault, he wouldn't challenge me, not when I was the one covering for him, out of the goodness of my heart."

Richard gives a laugh, and I'm chilled to the core. He talks about killing children in the same tone as ordering champagne. I want to get the fuck away from him as soon as possible, but I can't help lingering, driven to uncover the whole truth.

"And that's why you staged the explosion on the jet?" I prompt, "And killed Brian Kendall? To stop me asking any more questions after exposing what I thought happened."

"You outlived your use to me," Richard replies. "As long as all signs pointed to my nephew being behind the wheel, I could let you play your little games with him. But having you digging around in the past wasn't worth the risk. The trail needed to end with Sebastian. So the fact he joined you on that flight... Well, that was just a fortunate bonus to me."

He pauses, narrowing his eyes. "Where is he, anyway?"

"You'll see," I reply, moving towards the door. It's time to leave, and get back to the safety of the party, but before I make it even two steps, Richard grabs a golf club from the bag by the bookcase, and strikes me, hard across the back of the legs.

Pain slams through me and I crumple, my purse skittering across the floor as I hit the ground.

"Did you really think I would simply let you walk out that door, after everything I just told you?" Richard stands over me, wielding the gold club with a truly deranged smirk on his face. "Tsk, Avery, I'm surprised. I thought you were smarter than that."

He swings it again, striking me hard in the stomach, and I wail in agony.

*Oh God.*

"I hit the links every weekend," he remarks, almost conversational as I sob there on the ground. "Excellent handicap. Keeps a man in fighting shape."

I curl in a ball, gasping for air. The pain is dizzying, radiating through my entire body, and I swear, he's broken my ribs. But almost as bad as the pain is the fear that sweeps through me, as I realize in horror that he's right.

I should have been smarter. I didn't see this coming.

Somehow, I thought that Richard wouldn't get his own hands dirty. That the public party would protect me.

That he wouldn't beat me to death on his office floor with his wife and half of England's elite sipping champagne just a few feet away.

I panic.

"Help!" I scream, struggling to crawl towards my purse.

The panic button is just inside. I need to warn Sebastian. "Someone help me!"

"That won't save you." Richard kicks the bag away, out of reach. "This office was built to my specifications. It's sound-proofed, with one-way glass."

He raises the club again, and I let out a cry. "Don't! Please!"

He smirks. "You know, since everyone already thinks you're dead... Nobody will mind if I kill you twice."

*Fuck.*

I force myself to my feet, lunging at him with a desperate cry as he swings. I manage to duck the impact of the club, and tackle him, crashing back against the desk. We go sprawling to the ground, and he loses his grip on the club.

Suddenly, there's a pounding on the door. "Avery!"

It's Sebastian!

Richard is distracted for a split-second, and I look wildly around for a weapon.

There. I see a letter opener gleaming on the rug. I dive for it and bring it up in a wild slash across his face.

"You bitch!"

Richard lets out a howl, as the blade catches his cheek. Blood sprays, and he stumbles back.

"Sebastian!" I scream. I turn and try to run for the door, but Richard hurls himself after me, tackling me to the floor.

His weight is suffocating, pressing down on my damaged torso, and I struggle to get free, but Richard is too heavy. Too strong. He grabs my wrist and pries the letter opener from my grip. I hold on tight, flailing desperately, but he suddenly bites down on my hand, and I instinctively flex in pain, releasing the blade.

Richard has it to my throat in an instant, the sharp edge pressing into my skin.

"I hope he was worth it," he growls, pressing harder.

Drawing blood. "I thought you hated him, too. Now you'll die for him."

*Oh god.* I wait for the killer slash, but then there's a deafening crash, and Sebastian hurtles into the room, breaking the door from its hinges.

"Avery!" he yells, dragging Richard off me, before he can land the final blow.

*Thank God!*

But my relief is short-lived, as Richard turns his fury—and the blade—on Sebastian, slashing wildly at him as the two men crash across the room.

"Sebastian!" I cry, terrified, watching them fight. It's a blur of limbs and blade, and even though Sebastian is stronger and more agile, Richard has madness in his eyes.

"Why the fuck can't you just STAY DEAD!" Richard screams, launching himself at Sebastian with a howl. The men stumble back, crashing straight into the glass wall. The windows shatter, and give way, and I watch in horror as they teeter there on the ledge.

"Sebastian!" I cry, diving after them. I grab his arm just in time, managing to swing his weight back—

As Richard plummets to the stone terrace below.

He lands with a sickening crack, and screams erupt from the partygoers, panicking at the sight.

Richard lays, splayed there on the ground. Eyes wide, and empty. Body crumpled.

The man is dead.

## Chapter 23

### *Avery*

"I'm fine!" I protest, trying to brush away the attentions of a paramedic. It doesn't take long for the party to be shut down, and the place flooded with police and ambulances. Now, people are milling around outside, gawking at all the drama, as a medic tries to tend to me in the back of an ambulance. "Really, don't worry about me."

"Of course they're worried," Sebastian looms over us, scowling. "You're black and blue."

"It's just bruising," I reassure him, wincing as the paramedic straps a bandage to my injured ribs. "They'll heal soon enough."

"She's right," the paramedic agrees. "There's nothing for it but rest. No more encounters with any golf clubs," he adds, straightening up.

"Believe me, she's staying on strict bed rest," Sebastian vows. "I'm not letting her out of my sight."

The paramedic moves on, and I shudder, still shocked with how close I came to real harm. If Richard had swung that club even one more time... If Sebastian hadn't broken the door down when he did...

"How did you know to come for me?" I ask, gazing up at him. He's bruised too, with a nasty cut on his arm, but of course, he waved off any medical attention after he dealt with the police. Thanks to my video of the whole confrontation, they quickly backed off coming after either of us. "I couldn't reach the panic button."

Sebastian's gaze darkens. "You were up there too long," he replies. "I just knew something was wrong. I could feel it in my gut."

"Well, I appreciate your gut," I say, trying to joke. But my words feel hollow, and Sebastian immediately draws me close.

"Owww!" I protest.

"Shit." He loosens his hold. "I'm sorry. But I meant what I said. I'm not letting you out of my sight again."

I exhale, restored by the safety of his embrace. "Good," I murmur softly. "Because I have no intention of leaving you either."

I pause, noticing the turmoil in his eyes. Guilt. He's carried enough of it in his life. I don't want him haunted by tonight.

"You are worth it," I whisper softly. "What Richard said, before? I don't care what danger comes along with us; you'll always be worth it to me."

Sebastian scowls. "There'll be no more danger," he says fiercely, and I smile at that. "I mean it, Avery. This is over now. Behind us. I promise, nobody will hurt you again."

I nod, worn out. "Nothing but blue skies and yachts?" I ask hopefully.

"And all the pina coladas you can drink," Sebastian promises, holding me gently.

I savor his embrace, the truth finally sinking past my shock and pain.

It's over.

Sebastian's past, Richard's vendetta. My own tangled quest for vengeance.

It's finally all behind us now, and for the first time, I can believe in that bright future Sebastian is promising, with no more lies or betrayal to hold us back.

A wretched sob cuts through the noise. I turn. It's Sebastian's mother, Trudy, being comforted by an officer, as Richard's body is covered in a plain sheet there on the ground. She looks devastated, and I can only imagine what she's feeling after all the revelations of the night.

I look to Sebastian. "Do you want to talk to her?" I murmur.

He pauses. "Not tonight. She's in shock. Once it's all had a chance to sink in, maybe we can sit down, and talk it through. She really had no idea," he says sadly. "It's going to take her a while to come to terms with the truth."

I squeeze his hand. I know there's distance between them, after years of her affection for Richard, but I'm hoping that in the end, they can repair their relationship. "And Scarlett is safe now," I say, relieved. "She can relax and go home to recover."

Sebastian nods. "I already called her. She's shocked at the news, but I think she's relieved, too. That I'm not the villain they were all telling her I was."

"You're the hero of the story now," I say, only half-kidding. Already, reporters are buzzing around, and I know it'll take only a few words to my journalist contact, Lulu, before Sebastian is splashed all over the front pages. Returned from the dead to reclaim his former glory. A story like this will make waves, for sure, and I'm glad that Sebastian's reputation will finally be restored.

"That doesn't matter," Sebastian shakes his head impatiently at the idea of scandal and status. "All that matters is you're safe now."

"We both are," I correct him, smiling in relief and gratitude. I take a deep breath, and then pause, realizing I have absolutely no idea what to do now. "What happens next?" I ask.

"You mean, now that we're not in exile, living under false identities and hunting to bring down a killer?" Sebastian replies, a smile on his lips.

I laugh. "Yeah, how about that."

"It's your choice," he tells me, leaning in for a slow, tender kiss. "Say the word, and it's yours."

I think about it, and then start to smile. "Any chance you can get your hands on another jet?"

## Chapter 24

### *Avery*

Paradise. Growing up the way I did, I never gave the word a second thought. After all, there's nothing heavenly about being raised in the mafia world, a place of violence and fear, spending every day on edge to stay one step ahead of danger.

But when Sebastian said I could have anything in the world, he meant it. And after the hell we've been through for the past few months, there's nothing I wanted more than this:

A private yacht bobbing gently on the ocean. Blue skies overhead. And nothing but aquamarine water for miles around, all the way to the horizon.

Bliss.

I sigh with happiness, laying back on the plush cushioned prow of the boat. After the news of Richard's death broke, England was a madhouse of press, and police, and breathless speculation. Sebastian's PR team took care of making sure everyone knew the truth about what had happened, but we didn't want to stick around to deal with the drama. In time, I'm guessing some other big scandal will replace him on the front pages, but until then, I'm happy to avoid the whole mess.

Now, we're a thousand miles away from all of it. The sun burns at the edges of my massive hat, toasting my skin with warmth until the icy fear that I felt with Richard is just a distant memory.

"Careful, you don't want to burn."

I sit up, as Sebastian joins me, wearing only swim trunks, and carrying two icy glasses. I smile, admiring the view. "My personal sunscreen assistant must be slipping," I coo, taking a sip of the delicious cocktail.

"My mistake." Sebastian gives me a wolfish grin. "I've fallen behind schedule. Let me make it up to you, immediately."

I pass him the sunscreen, and turn my back, as he squeezes a dollop of the cool cream, and slowly smooths it over my shoulders.

"Nero and Lily texted," I report, glancing back at him. "They want to meet you, if we stop by in New York. Properly, I mean," I add with a grin. "No vendettas or corporate takeovers allowed."

Sebastian snorts with laughter. "Sure, we'll all get dinner. In fact, why not invite Caleb and Juliet, too?" he adds, naming Nero's half-brother—and another of Sebastian's bitter rivals. "Since we're all as good as family now."

I giggle at the idea. The mafia boss, the jewelry CEO, and the corporate raider, under one roof. We would have to scan for weapons at the door, after everything they've been through. "Now that would be an interesting night!"

My laughter turns to a gasp as his touch becomes deliberate, skating over my bare skin, down to my bikini strings.

"Now, what did I tell you about the boat rules?" he murmurs, tugging at the ties.

"That you wanted me naked at all times?" I laugh, turning back to him. "Sebastian, you can't be serious—"

He tugs the ties, and my bikini top falls away. "I never joke when it comes to your body," he says, with an appreciative growl. "Now, you need to pay a forfeit to the captain."

"Yes, sir," I tease, and arch my back, inviting. "Come claim your prize."

His eyes blaze over my bare breasts, and then he's leaning in, dipping his head to kiss one slope, his mouth dragging over the sensitive skin.

I moan, sinking back. Sebastian sucks one nipple into his mouth, moving me to lay beneath him. His erection is already pressing thickly against me, and I whimper in anticipation, grinding up to tease him, just the way he's driving me crazy.

Sebastian groans, lifting his head. "You're insatiable," he smirks, and I grin back. We've been making love nonstop all week; we couldn't even wait until the flight touched down before making good use of his jet's private bedroom.

"Are you complaining?"

"Never," he vows, nipping at one earlobe. "In fact, I thank God every minute of every day that I have you here, all to myself."

"That's a lot of gratitude," I bite my lip, giving him a look as, deliberately, I part my thighs. "Show me."

Sebastian's eyes flash with lust. "With pleasure."

He hooks his thumbs over my bikini bottoms and tugs them down. I don't know why I bothered to even put them on; Sebastian has kept me naked pretty much constantly since we set sail.

Naked, and gasping his name.

Now, he settles between my legs, and gives my pussy a lazy lick, making me tense and gasp in pleasure before slowly, teasingly, he begins to lap at my aching clit.

"Oh…" I sink back, my moans of pleasure echoing across the water.

"Louder, baby," Sebastian urges me on. "Let's see if they can hear you on dry land."

I laugh—and quickly shift to a cry, as he toys and sucks, slipping one finger, then two, deep into my wetness to pulse and flex in time with his wicked tongue. "*Seb!*"

"Better," he growls, licking me into a frenzy right there on the deck of the boat. It truly feels like we're the only people in the world, out here on the calm ocean, our days filled with laughter, and lazy talks, and *this*.

All of this.

"Oh God… There…. *Yes!*"

Pleasure ripples through me. Sebastian brings me to a swift climax with his hands and mouth, nipping on my thigh as my body shakes. I lift my head, breathless. "If that's what I get for breaking the boat rules, you're not exactly giving me incentive to obey," I say with a satisfied smile.

Sebastian gazes down at me, still heated. "Oh, you'll do what I tell you, Sparrow," he says with a dark smirk. "We both know, you'll do anything to be my good girl."

My stomach curls with delicious lust.

"Make me," I whisper, and his eyes flash.

"You sure about that?"

He doesn't even wait for a reply, before scooping me over his shoulder, striding to the prow of the boat, and leaping—right into the cold ocean.

SPLASH!

We hit the water, and I shriek at the shock of cool water against my naked skin. I surface, spluttering. "Oh, you'll pay for that!" I giggle, recovering as I tread water. Sebastian is splashing nearby and sends a shower of water in my direction.

"Try your worst!"

We splash each other, laughing, until Sebastian sweeps me closer in his arms, and claims my mouth in a sizzling kiss. I relax into his embrace, reveling in the feel of his hot mouth, and the cool water, the perfect contrasts—just like him. Dark intensity, and this new playful side that Sebastian is showing me more with every passing day.

More to love.

"I wish we could stay here forever," I sigh happily, as he treads water, keeping us both afloat.

"That's my plan," Sebastian grins back. "At least, until you grow bored with me."

"Bored of this? Never," I vow, wrapping my legs around his waist. His cock presses against my core, and I press closer, biting down on his lower lip. "I could fuck you forever," I whisper. "And love you even longer."

Sebastian growls against me, his grip tightens. "Then let's do both. Always."

Back onboard, Sebastian practically drags me down to the luxurious cabin, and throws me on the bed with a bounce. "I mean it," he says, prowling closer. Magnificent. "I don't ever want to lose you."

"You won't." My breath catches, seeing him there above me. Dark and glorious, flawed and perfect, all at once.

The man I swore I'd destroy.

The man I've grown to love more than life itself.

I could never have predicted that my journey would take me here, with him, but now we're together, I can't imagine anything more perfect.

Sebastian looks down at me, his eyes full of emotion. "So marry me."

My jaw drops. I can't believe I've heard him right.

"What?"

"Marry me," Sebastian insists again. "Be mine. Forever. Because my heart is yours, my Sparrow. It's always been yours."

Emotion overwhelms me. "Yes!" I blurt, reaching for him. "Oh my God, yes!"

I kiss him, fevered, my mind dizzy with the sense of possibility.

The two of us. Together. Always.

Sebastian groans against my mouth, and then he pulls back, passion blazing in his eyes. "Forever," he vows. He grips my knees in each hand, and yanks me to the edge of the bed, positioning himself there, his cock hard and straining for me.

"Forever," I echo, as he thrusts into me, hard, and sweet, and *fuck*, so deep it makes me sob with pleasure. And I take him, every inch, begging for more with wild abandon.

This is where I belong. Where I'll always be.

And as our cries ring out over the water, I've never felt more complete.

## THE END

Thank you for reading!

If you'd like to see what happens when Avery, Sebastian, Nero, Lily, Juliet and Caleb get together for that dinner… Sign up for my newsletter, to claim your special bonus epilogue, featuring all the characters!

**Visit my website at www.roxysloane.com to claim your bonus epilogue**.

*New from Roxy Sloane comes a spicy dark academia romance trilogy...*

The Oxford Legacy: Book One
CROSS MY HEART

'*Oxford, England. The city of dreaming spires, dark secrets... And desire.*'
**Discover the sizzling dark academia romance series by USA Today Bestselling author, Roxy Sloane - perfect for fans of Ana Huang, Emily McIntire, and Lauren Asher.**

Anthony St Clair. The future Duke of Ashford.

A reckless enigma... and my greatest temptation.

I came here on a mission, to uncover the truth about what happened to my sister - no matter the cost.

Until I meet him.

Saint is my passport to a sensual world of wealth and privilege, but something wicked is lurking behind these ivy covered walls.

Secrets these people will kill to protect.

Loyalty is everything to them... but will it be my ruin?

THE OXFORD LEGACY TRILOGY:
1. Cross My Heart
2. Break My Rules
3. Seal My Fate

Roxy Sloane is a USA Today bestselling author, with over 2 million books sold world-wide. She loves writing page-turning spicy romance full of captivatingly alpha heroes, sensual passion, and a sprinkle of glamor. She lives in Los Angeles, and enjoys shocking whoever looks at her laptop screen when she writes in local coffee shops.

\* \* \*

**To get free books, news and more, sign up to my VIP list!**

www.roxysloane.com
roxy@roxysloane.com

Printed in Great Britain
by Amazon

46812376R00116